The temptation of being too close

Erin sat staring into the fire, her features soft and fragile in the flickering light. She reminded Nick of a painting he'd once seen—pale, innocent, with an almost mystical aura. But unmistakably woman.

Another time, he would have leaned over and kissed her. He would have taken his time, tasting her delicate lips, loosening her hair until it fell wantonly down her back. He would have touched her all over, whispered what he wanted to do to her...

He let the fantasy spin away with no small regret, and turned his attention back to the darkness outside the cabin. A murderer was out there waiting, and since Nick had been the one to drag Erin into this mess, it was his duty to protect her, not to seduce her.

But Nick knew that one sometimes led almost inevitably to the other...

Forbidden Lover

AMANDA STEVENS

SILHOUETTE INTRIGUE

*First published in Great Britain 2000
Silhouette Books, Eton House, 18-24 Paradise Road,
Richmond, Surrey TW9 1SR*

© Marilyn Medlock Amann 2000

ISBN 0 373 22557 1

46-1000

*Printed and bound in Spain
by Litografia Rosés S.A., Barcelona*

ABOUT THE AUTHOR

Amanda Stevens has written over twenty novels of romantic suspense. Her books have appeared on several best-seller lists, and she has won Reviewer's Choice and Career Achievement in Romantic/Mystery awards from *Romantic Times Magazine*. She resides in Cypress, Texas, with her husband, her son and daughter, and their two cats.

Dear Reader,

Welcome! Here's a quick glimpse at what's available this month in Silhouette Intrigue®.

Amanda Stevens's splendidly passionate trilogy GALLAGHER JUSTICE draws to a close. At last you can discover what really happened to Sean Gallagher in *Forbidden Lover*, Nick's story. And if you're fond of men who uphold the law and protect the innocent, don't miss this month's LAWMAN LOVER novel, *A Woman of Mystery*.

Paige Roberts wakes up to find she can't remember the last six weeks of her life in this month's AMNESIA book, *The Baby Secret*. Paige discovers she's pregnant, but...*who's the father?*

Finally, a plane crash brings old flames back together, despite there being a killer hidden among the handful of survivors; that's *When Night Draws Near*, a first Intrigue™ from Lisa Bingham.

Enjoy,

The Editors

Chapter One

The bones talked to her while she worked. As Dr. Erin Casey painstakingly examined the human cranium on her worktable, the story of a life began to unfold for her.

The skull was small and lightweight, which told her the remains were female, and the width of the hipbone concurred. Further examination revealed a small indentation on the pubic bone, indicating that the woman had given birth to at least two children.

The unidentified female was someone's mother.

How old were her children? Did they still wonder what had happened to their mother? Did they sometimes lie in bed at night, missing her so badly they ached? Did they still dream about her?

Behind her goggles, Erin's eyes closed briefly as an image of her own mother flitted through her mind. She'd been dead for nearly a year now, but sometimes the loss still seemed too much for Erin to bear. Sometimes the urge to talk to her mother was so strong, the need so great, that Erin would find herself lifting the phone to her ear, only to realize all over again that if she dialed her mother's number, a stranger would undoubtedly pick up.

Madeline Casey had been everything to Erin—a devoted mother, a best friend, a trusted confidante. The two of them had been on their own from the time Erin was just a baby, moving from city to city for the first few years of her life, running, she now knew, from a past that had colored her life in ways she was only beginning to understand.

Perhaps that was why she'd accepted a faculty position at Hillsboro University, a small, private college in Chicago, the city where Erin had been born and where her mother had grown up. Erin had family here, but none of them would recognize her if they met her on the street or heard her name. She hadn't seen any of them, including her father, since she was nine months old, nor they her. And Erin's mother had long ago legally changed both their names, not so much for safety's sake—though that had undoubtedly been a consideration—but in an effort to sever all ties with a family that had been morally and legally corrupt.

Erin felt no bitterness about the separation. She understood her mother's motives all too well. The reason she'd moved back to Chicago had nothing to do with renewing ties with her father or his family. Far from it.

She'd come here solely because of her mother. From the moment the offer from Hillsboro had been presented to her, Erin had sensed her mother's presence would be strong here. Madeline had grown up in Chicago, gone to school and fallen in love here. She'd married and given birth to two children here. When she'd moved away, she'd left a part of her heart behind, and in some strange way, Erin knew this was where she would finally find a sense of herself, here in the shadow of her mother's past.

And, of course, the state-of-the-art laboratory of which Erin was in charge had played no small part in her decision. Funded almost entirely by a wealthy, anonymous donor, the Forensic Anthropology and Human Identification Laboratory, usually referred to as FAHIL, rivaled the one at the University of Tennessee, where Erin had received her doctorate in physical anthropology and where the famous "body farm" was located.

All in all, she considered her move to Chicago from the sometimes sweltering climate of Knoxville to be a wise one. The campus was small with the usual petty jealousies and academic backstabbing, but in the two months that Erin had been on staff, her reception had been fairly warm. She suspected the ease with which she had been accepted had more to do with the reputation she'd earned at the Anthropological Research Facility in Knoxville than with her personally.

As one of only a handful of board-certified forensic anthropologists nationwide, her presence at Hillsboro was something of a coup. Her name had quickly been added to the Chicago Police Department's consultation list, as well as law enforcement agencies all over Illinois and the Midwest. Hillsboro's board of trustees were very aware that a high-profile case could bring donors out of the woodwork.

Case 00-03, the unidentified mother on Erin's worktable, was her third consultation with CPD, and though it didn't promise to be high-profile, there was something about the woman's remains that had captured Erin's imagination.

The skeleton had been discovered less than a week ago, beneath an old house that was being torn down in Chinatown. Erin hadn't been invited to examine the skeleton in situ, but instead, the remains had been dug up and transported in a black plastic bag to the pathology lab at the Chicago Technology Park. The pathologist on duty had quickly concluded there wasn't enough tissue remaining on the bones for an autopsy to be of much use, so Erin had been called in.

Carefully, she took facial measurements, narrating her findings for the video camera that recorded every nuance of her examination. The notes would later be transcribed and included in the report she would give to the police.

The broad face, squared winglike cheekbones, and small low-bridged nasal bone were characteristics of the Mongoloid race. Since the skeleton had been found in Chinatown, Erin knew there was a very good chance the remains were Asian.

An Asian mother of at least two children.

The story continued to unfold.

Next, Erin began to determine the woman's age by studying the degree of fusion in the femur, the closure of the cranial sutures, and the—

"Dr. Casey?"

Absorbed in her work, Erin jumped at the unexpected sound of a human voice. The bones talked to her, but they never spoke out loud.

She glanced up. Gloria Maynard, her secretary, stood tentatively inside the lab door, her expression wary. She didn't like coming down here. The shelved bones and skulls patiently awaiting identification made her nervous, but then death made a lot of people nervous. But not Erin. If anything, she took comfort in the knowledge that stripped of skin, tissue, and muscle, human beings were all pretty much the same underneath.

Including the tall, good-looking man who hovered outside in the hallway, just beyond the open door.

Erin frowned. She didn't like strangers invading her private domain, for security reasons among others. "What's going on?" she asked Gloria.

The secretary glanced over her shoulder. In spite of her discomfort, her eyes danced excitedly. "There's a detective outside to see you. I told him to wait in your office, but he insisted on coming down here. He said he needed to talk to you about an urgent case—"

The man pushed past Gloria into the lab, as if too impatient to wait any longer. Erin didn't much care for his attitude, but whoever he was, he certainly had excellent bone structure, she'd give him that. She automatically cataloged his features. Wide shoulders, narrow waist, lean hips. Moving to his face, she noted the high cheekbones, the well-defined brow, and the piercing blue eyes, so striking against his dark coloring.

His impatience emanated from every nerve ending in his body. He looked incapable of standing still. He wore a sport coat with charcoal trousers, and his hand swept restlessly down his striped tie as his gaze roamed every nook and cranny of the lab, undisturbed, he would have her think, by the rows of human skulls grinning silently from the shelves.

Satisfied with what he'd seen, his blue gaze came back to rest on Erin. Her stomach fluttered, not from attraction or sexual awareness she was quite sure, but from apprehension. Somehow she knew the man's presence here in her lab did not bode well for her future peace of mind.

"So you're the bone lady," he said, in a voice deepened not so much by age—Erin judged him to be in his early thirties, possibly two or three years older than she—but by confidence and authority, a man who liked telling others what to do.

She bristled instantly. "No," she told him coolly. "I'm not the bone lady, although I thank you for the compliment. That moniker belongs to another forensic anthropologist, one I admire very much."

"Fair enough," he said easily, although his gaze seemed to intensify on her. "But you are Dr. Casey, aren't you? Dr. Erin Casey?"

"Yes." She shoved her goggles to the top of her head, then peeled off her gloves and disposed of them in the waste receptacle before she ventured across the room toward him. "And you are…?"

"Detective Gallagher," Gloria piped in, as if she had only now remembered his name. Her voice was higher than normal, and she couldn't seem to take her eyes off the man. "He's with the Chicago PD."

Detective Gallagher shot her a bemused glance. "Thanks, but I can take it from here."

A blush sneaked up Gloria's neck, fascinating Erin. Outspoken, flirtatious, occasionally obnoxious, Gloria Maynard was not the type to embarrass easily, but Detective Gallagher had definitely flustered her. She seemed torn between wanting to escape from the lab, and hanging around long enough to somehow get his phone number.

"What can I do for you, Detective Gallagher?" Erin asked him.

He took a few steps into the lab. "Could we speak in private?"

The blush on Gloria's face deepened. "I'll be at my desk if you need me," she muttered, spinning on her heel and closing the door with a soft thud behind her. Erin was fairly certain that Gloria wasn't used to being dismissed so curtly—at least not by a man. Her shiny black hair, short skirts, and tight sweaters usually drew lingering and longing stares from the male members of the faculty and student body alike. But Detective Gallagher didn't even seem to take notice of her leaving. Erin warmed to him a little.

"We're alone now," she said, then felt her own face color at the suggestive way she'd phrased her observation. She pulled down her goggles and plunked them on her nose as she turned back to her worktable. "Mind if I work while we talk?"

"Not at all, as long as I have your attention." Detective Gallagher walked around the table, so that they were facing each other. Erin drew on a fresh pair of latex gloves and handed him a pair. "Just in case you get curious."

Reluctantly, he took the gloves. Erin had never understood the mindset of police officers who could work bloody crime and accident scenes so coolly and calmly, but then grew uneasy—some downright green—at the sight of skeletal remains. Detective Gallagher didn't particularly strike her as the squeamish type, but he did seem to have a healthy respect for his surroundings.

At any rate, the bones spread over Erin's worktable were nearly pristine. All that remained were the clues that would unravel the woman's identity and cause of death.

"Do you know who she is yet?"

Erin glanced up in surprise. "How did you know it's a she?"

He shrugged. "I've learned a few things over the years. So, who is she and what happened to her?" His tone was faintly challenging.

"I haven't finished my examination," Erin said almost irritably.

"Oh, come on." His blue gaze taunted her. "Your reputation precedes you, Dr. Casey. According to Dr. Wyman, your abilities are nothing short of mystical."

Erin had met Dr. Lawrence Wyman, the Cook County Medical Examiner, a couple of years ago at a conference in New York. They'd hit it off, spent several hours together, and since then had kept in touch by e-mail. He'd been ecstatic when he'd learned she was moving to Chicago.

"Did Dr. Wyman send you here?" Erin asked.

"Like I said, you come highly recommended."

She frowned at his evasion. "What kind of case do you want me to consult on?"

He nodded toward the skeleton. "Tell me about her first."

A test, Erin thought. He wanted to see for himself how good she was. Not that she needed to prove anything to him, but Erin began reciting in a monotone everything she had learned from the bones. "She gave birth to at least two children. Mongoloid, more than likely Asian. Height, around five feet. Weight, around 110, 115..." she trailed off, examining the muscle attachment markings on the tibia.

"Anything else?" Detective Gallagher quizzed her.

"She was a fairly accomplished athlete. A runner, I'd say." Erin smiled slightly. "And of course, she was murdered."

ERIN CASEY was a strange little woman, not at all what Nick had expected. He studied the framed diplomas, certifications and professional affiliations on her office wall with half his attention while the other half tried to reconcile his preconceived image of her with the actual person.

For one thing, she was a lot younger than he'd imagined. Dr. Wyman was in his sixties, but he'd spoken of Erin Casey with the reverence and respect usually reserved for one's contemporaries and elders. He doubted she was even thirty, and her slight stature made her seem even younger. Nick was willing to bet she was often mistaken for a student on campus, although her intensity, her almost trancelike absorption in her work was far from juvenile. She was good at what she did. She was very, very good.

Not only had she determined that the subject on her worktable had been murdered, but also that she was likely a runner, an important detail because the habits of a victim could often lead back to the killer.

Nick needed that same resourcefulness and intuition, that same thoroughness, to tell him if the remains that had been discovered yesterday were also those of a murder victim. And, of course, he needed the identity of the dead man. But if he turned out to be who Nick suspected he was...

His thoughts broke apart and scattered. He wouldn't allow himself to think about that. Not yet. First things first. Excavate the remains. Bring them here to Dr. Casey's lab. Let her work her magic. And then Nick would take over from there.

He felt the rage building inside him again at the injustice that was about to be perpetrated by the legal system, but he couldn't let his anger take control of him. Too much was at stake. A murderer was about to go free, but the discovery of the skeleton yesterday could change everything.

If Daniel O'Roarke's death sentence for the brutal

slaying eight years ago of a beautiful, young coed was overturned, he could never again be tried for her murder. But if he'd killed again...if the remains of his second victim suddenly turned up after eight long years of searching...he could be sent back to death row, this time for killing a cop.

The door of the office opened, and Nick felt his nerve endings jump slightly. He was edgy and he knew it, but he'd never worked on a case this important. This personal. And because of the potential for publicity—and danger—discretion was a primary concern. Could he trust Erin Casey?

Dr. Wyman seemed to think so. "The woman's as honorable as she is brilliant. A very rare combination," he'd mused wistfully.

The old man was probably half in love with her, Nick decided, as he gazed at Erin Casey with a new eye. He supposed she was attractive, in a scholarly, nondescript sort of way. She was tiny, probably not much over five feet, and Nick doubted she'd weigh more than a hundred pounds soaking wet.

Her hair was dark blond, and she wore the long, wavy strands pulled back and twisted into a thick braid that thumped against her back when she walked. The wire-rimmed glasses perched on her nose made her light-blue eyes appear huge and misty and gave her a dreamlike quality that seemed almost otherworldly. Her skin was smooth and pale, as if she spent most of her time bent over a worktable in her basement lab instead of out in the sunshine with the rest of the human race.

She looked freshly showered, having changed from the disposable scrubs into jeans and a yellow cotton shirt that had an ink stain on the front. Nick was willing to bet she hadn't even noticed the stain, and if she had, she wouldn't care anyway. Appearance was obviously not high on her priority list, and yet, she managed to convey a kind of absentminded sensuality that she would undoubtedly find surprising, and Nick found more than a little disturbing.

She sat down behind her desk and gazed up at him. "Have a seat, Detective Gallagher."

He didn't want to sit, but it would be rude not to, and besides, his pacing drove most people crazy. The only other chair in the room was stacked with books and papers, and she gave a careless, sweeping wave, which Nick took as permission to transfer the heap to the floor.

When he was finally seated, he could feel the impatience burning inside him again, mingling with the raw energy flowing almost like a drug through his veins. They had to get moving on this, he kept thinking over and over. There was no time to waste.

"Tell me about the remains you've found." Her soft, southern accent was discordant with the topic of their conversation. Her voice came straight from the pages of *Gone with the Wind*. But there was nothing fragile or coy about Erin Casey.

"A hunter found the bones yesterday morning," he told her. "In a remote, wooded area in Wisconsin."

Her brows lifted slightly over the rim of her glasses. "Hardly CPD's jurisdiction, is it?"

"No, but I know the county sheriff in that area. He called me when the remains were discovered."

"Why?" Her blue eyes behind the glasses were gently probing.

Nick frowned at her persistence. "He doesn't want any publicity until he has a handle on what he's dealing with."

"You mean until he learns whether the bones are forensic or archaeological?"

"Yes, but his concern is even more basic than that. It looks like a human skeleton, but who knows?" Nick shrugged. "Remember that case down south a few years ago where a man digging in a flower bed in his backyard uncovered several coffinlike boxes that contained what the local authorities thought were the skeletal remains of infants? The sheriff even went so far as to call in the FBI, thinking he had some kind of gruesome serial killer on his hands. Turned out the previous owners of the house had used that spot for their pet cemetery. The remains were a dog, two cats, and a canary. The media had a field day with that poor sheriff and his deputies."

"Actually, I do remember that case," Erin said. "I'm the one who examined the bones."

"No kidding?" Nick had already known that, of course, but he thought it was a good way to make his point. "Anyway, my friend would like you to come up and take a look at the remains, see what you think."

"Where is the skeleton now?"

"Exactly where it was found. We want you to oversee the excavation."

"I see." She was intrigued by the prospect, Nick could tell. Too often, remains were sent prematurely to the pathology lab or to the morgue before a proper excavation and search of the area were conducted.

"The sooner you excavate, the better," she murmured, glancing at the calendar on her desk. "If it rains, crucial evidence could be washed away, but unfortunately, I'm completely tied up until Wednesday."

Two days away, Nick calculated. And the weather

service predicted a major rainstorm in the next twenty-four hours.

"Can't you rearrange your schedule?" he urged. "The time factor could be critical here."

"But you don't even know whether the remains are human or not."

He met her gaze. "They're human."

"But you just said—"

"I said the sheriff up there doesn't want to come off looking like some kind of fool, which is true. He's not sure the remains are human, but I am."

"You've seen them?"

"I drove up yesterday as soon as he called me. We're trying to keep this as quiet as possible, but in case word leaks out, a couple of deputies are patrolling the area. Just between you and me, though, I'm not sure how effective that precaution will be. They were all pretty spooked by the discovery, and I doubt any of them were willing to spend the night in those woods last night."

"I understand." She frowned at her calendar, as if mentally juggling her schedule. "But I'm afraid there's no way I can get up there before tomorrow. I have classes the rest of the day, and…" her frown deepened momentarily "…an engagement tonight that I can't possibly get out of…"

Her words trailed off, and Nick wondered if the engagement she couldn't get out of tonight was a social one. Did she have a date? If so, she didn't look all that keen on going, so what was the problem?

"I could wait around and drive you up as soon as you're finished," he suggested. "We could start the excavation at first light tomorrow."

"If you're in that much of a hurry, perhaps you

should try someone else. Who did CPD use before I moved to Chicago?''

''Dr. Bernard Rosenbaum, but he's laid up with a broken leg. Dr. Ernesto Gonzalez occasionally backs up Rosenbaum, but he lives over two hundred miles away, and besides, he's working in Bosnia right now. There's no one else available, Dr. Casey. And it's going to rain tomorrow afternoon,'' he stressed. ''I need you up there as soon as possible.''

Something in his tone must have conveyed his urgency, because she looked up, letting her blue gaze rest on him for the longest moment before she nodded almost imperceptibly. ''All right. I'll see if I can rearrange my schedule. But you don't have to wait around for me. Just leave me your number and I'll call you tonight when I'm finished.''

He stood, fishing a card from his pocket and dropping it on her desk. ''If it's all the same with you, I think I'll hang around campus for a while anyway.''

''That really isn't necessary—''

''Look…'' He shot a glance toward the door. ''I'm a little concerned about security. If you wouldn't mind, I'd like to take a look at your facility.''

''Security? For remains that haven't yet been identified as human?''

When he said nothing, her gaze grew mildly reproachful. ''There's something you're not telling me about this case.''

''I've told you everything I know about the remains.''

''Then why are you so concerned about security?''

''Security is my job. In case you haven't thought about it before, you've got a murder victim lying in your lab downstairs. Someone out there isn't going to be too thrilled when you ID her.''

She didn't seem the least bit fazed by his words. ''This building is equipped with a sophisticated security system, including highly sensitive motion detectors. A special lock was designed for the lab doors, and only a few of the FAHIL staff have been issued keys. The doors to the FAHIL facilities are kept locked at night, and the building has its own security guard. Does that sound satisfactory to you?''

Her thoroughness impressed him once more. ''You would have made a very good detective, Dr. Casey.''

Again, she gave him a slight smile, but her tone was deadly serious. ''But I am a detective. I'm a bone detective. I just don't carry a gun.''

And if she did carry a gun, Nick had no doubt she would be a crack shot. He had a feeling there were very few things Dr. Erin Casey didn't do well.

The possibilities, he decided, were pretty damn intriguing.

''DR. CASEY! Wait up!''

Erin, balancing her briefcase, an armload of books and papers, and a can of highly caffeinated soda, turned at the sound of her name. Ross Calvert, her research assistant, hurried up the sidewalk toward her.

''I'm glad I caught you, Dr. Casey,'' Ross said breathlessly as he drew alongside her.

''I'm in a bit of a hurry, Ross, so whatever this is about, can it wait?'' He looked instantly crestfallen, and Erin cursed herself for her curt tone. ''I'm sorry. It's just that I have that reception tonight at the dean's house, and you know how much I hate those things.''

Ross nodded sympathetically, his normal good humor somewhat restored. He wore baggy black jeans, a black Primus T-shirt, and his dyed hair had been gelled into orangy-red spikes. The grunge look, including the eyebrow ring and chin stud, belied his keen intelligence. He was one of the sharpest research assistants Erin had ever had.

"You'll be cool," he said admiringly.

"I appreciate that, Ross. Now, what can I do for you?"

He hesitated, then said, "There was a man in the lab this afternoon working on Case 00-03 with you." His gaze lifted suddenly, and his gray eyes had an oddly possessive glint.

Erin thought she understood. Case 00-03 was to be Ross's solo project. Once Erin had cataloged her findings, he would then conduct his own examination, comparing his conclusions with hers. One always felt possessive of one's first case, she reminisced nostalgically. "*I* was working on 00-03," she told him. "Detective Gallagher was merely observing."

"Detective Gallagher? He's not the one who brought her to us. That cop's name was Stoner."

"Yes, that's right. Detective Mike Stoner."

"So, what did Gallagher want?"

It was Erin's turn to hesitate, remembering Detective Gallagher's almost excessive concern for security. "I think he wanted to look over the premises, make sure our security was up to snuff. Some of the remains we work on represent potential evidence in court cases," she reminded him. "A lot of good detective work could go down the drain if they were tampered with."

Ross didn't look all that convinced. "I guess that explains what *he* was doing here, but what about the other guy?"

"The other guy?"

"There was another man standing just outside the building, pretending to read a book," Ross told her. "He looked up when you came out, and he just stood there watching you walk away."

Erin suppressed a shiver at the notion of someone—anyone—surreptitiously watching her. Among other concerns, her backside was definitely not her best asset.

"What did he look like?" she asked Ross.

He shrugged. "I don't know. He was older, with sort of grayish hair. And he was big. Not fat, just…big. Muscular."

"What did he do after I walked away?"

"He got in his car and drove off. But I don't think he left the campus. I think he's still hanging around here somewhere."

Erin tried to shrug away his concern. "I'm sure it's nothing for either one of us to worry about. He was probably just waiting for someone."

"Maybe." Ross gave her a doubtful smile. "Just thought I'd mention it, though. I guess I'll see you tomorrow, Dr. Casey."

"See you tomorrow, Ross." Although she wasn't so sure she would, if she left tonight with Detective Gallagher. Depending on how long the excavation took, she might not be back until day after tomorrow, but for some reason, she didn't feel like mentioning that possibility to Ross. He worried too much.

As Erin watched him walk toward the parking lot, she remembered Detective Gallagher's warning about security. *In case you haven't thought about it before, you've got a murder victim lying in your lab downstairs. Someone out there is going to be awfully unhappy when you ID her.*

Did the strange man Ross had seen lurking about campus have something to do with Case 00-03?

Or was he somehow associated with Detective Gallagher?

Neither scenario was particularly comforting, and Erin suppressed another shiver as she turned to walk home. It was only September, but there was a bite in the wind off the lake that promised an early winter.

The days were getting shorter, too. The sun was already setting over the picturesque campus, casting long shadows between the ivy-covered buildings, and for the first time in years, the coming darkness made Erin more than a little uneasy.

Chapter Two

Dean Stanton was in rare form, Erin observed at the reception that night. A dour man with a much younger and more attractive wife, the head of Hillsboro University usually did well to string more than two or three sentences together without pausing to glower.

Tonight, however, he was almost ebullient, talking and laughing with the members of the board and faculty, going out of his way to make each and every one of them feel welcome.

There were several wealthy alumni in attendance as well, and Erin suspected their presence played heavily in the dean's exhibition of good humor.

Plus, it was obvious he enjoyed showing off his house and his wife, and who could blame him? They were both gorgeous, the latter being tall, blond, and buxom, with her rather impressive attributes stunningly displayed in a low-cut, ice-blue cocktail dress.

And the house was every bit her equal. The lower level was huge, with one room flowing into the next through high, arching doorways. Silk rugs dotted the polished hardwood floors, and the paneled walls and heavy oak shelving were garnished with oil paintings and African artifacts. Ornate chandeliers spilled soft lighting throughout the rooms, and a magnificent free-standing staircase curved gracefully to a second-floor gallery where another group of people mingled with drinks.

Erin had always imagined her father's home looking something like this—spacious and grand with evidence of the family's ill-gotten gains nearly everywhere one looked.

Dean Stanton had earned his house the old-fashioned way. It came with his title. A definite perk for climbing the academic ladder, Erin decided.

She stood apart from the throng, sipping her wine and eyeing the gathering with a bored, critical eye. Schmoozing with the board of trustees and would-be donors was a part of her work she hated, but it was necessary in her field, where laboratories and research grants were often funded by private donations.

Erin caught Dean Stanton's eye, and he motioned her over. He was talking to a particularly intense-looking group of people, and Erin grimaced inwardly as she made her way across the crowded room.

"I'd like you to meet the newest member of the Hillsboro family," he said proudly, his gaze moving over Erin in an appreciative sweep. She suspected he'd been worried about what she might turn up here wearing tonight, but in spite of her distaste for such functions, she'd learned a long time ago how to play the game.

She wore a black, sleeveless tunic over matching pants and a fluid silk jersey that clung to her scant curves, filling them out in ways nature had forgotten to. Her high heels helped alleviate nature's other slight, and just to remind herself that she hadn't been entirely forsaken, she'd left her hair down. The thick, wavy tresses swung over her shoulders, framing her face in a way that made her feel sexy and wanton. A fleeting feeling, to be sure...

She felt Dean Stanton's hand on her back, urging her into the spotlight, and Erin had to resist the temptation to pull back. He made the introductions, but the names all ran together in her head, and she hardly noticed any of the faces, except for the tall man who took her hand and held it for a shade longer than she would have liked.

He was impeccably dressed, with silver hair slicked back from his face and a dark tan that highlighted the coldest pair of gray eyes she'd ever encountered. There was something about those eyes, about the way he looked at her, that made Erin experience the same vague uneasiness she'd felt that afternoon after talking with Ross.

Could this man be the one Ross had seen watching her? He did look familiar, and even his name, Ed Dawson, rang a very faint bell.

Erin's stomach fluttered in warning as she removed her hand from his. She heard Dean Stanton address him again, and she listened more alertly, trying to place where she might have seen him before.

"...consulting on cases all over the Midwest as well as Chicago," Stanton was saying. He turned to Erin. "Why don't you tell us about some of the cases you worked on down in Knoxville, Dr. Casey?"

Erin frowned briefly, not wanting to talk about her work except in the most general terms. "Most of my work is fairly routine. Not all that interesting to anyone other than myself."

The silver-haired man's brows lifted slightly. "You're far too modest. I find what you do fascinating,

Dr. Casey. I'd certainly like to hear more about your cases at some future date, particularly the ones connected with the Chicago Police Department.''

"Those cases are current," she explained, "and may end up in court. I'm really not at liberty to discuss them."

Dean Stanton scowled at her. "Your reticence is admirable, Dr. Casey, but if the superintendent of the Chicago Police Department wants an update on the criminal cases in which you're currently involved, you would have no objection, surely."

Superintendent of the Chicago Police Department? Of course! That's why the man's face and name seemed so familiar. Undoubtedly, Erin had seen Ed Dawson on television, or perhaps seen his picture in the newspaper.

She glanced at him apologetically. "I'm sorry. But I was just reminded this afternoon how vital it is to safeguard our forensic work."

"No apology necessary," Dawson said smoothly. "As Dean Stanton correctly pointed out, your discretion is admirable. A cocktail party is not the place for such a discussion." The look he gave Dean Stanton was almost frigid, and Stanton, in turn, glared angrily at Erin. There was no mistaking who would get the blame for his faux pas.

Just then, a woman behind Ed Dawson turned and came to join them. She looked to be in her late fifties, probably around Dawson's age, but she was still a very pretty woman, with a nice complexion and short, dark hair. The green silk dress she wore was exactly right for her age and her coloring, and the smile she flashed Erin was the first genuine show of friendliness she'd seen all evening.

Ed Dawson took her hand and pulled her forward. "I'd like you to meet a good friend of mine. This is Maggie Gallagher," he said to the group, but his gaze remained on Erin. "She has three sons who are in the Detective Division. It's possible you may cross paths with one of them in the future, Dr. Casey."

Startled, Erin stared at the woman for a moment. Maggie Gallagher's features, especially her blue eyes, were very like the detective's Erin had met earlier that day. Were Dawson's words prophetic, or did he know Nick Gallagher had already been to see her?

She gave Maggie a tentative smile. "Very nice to meet you, Mrs. Gallagher."

"Call me Maggie," the woman said warmly.

"And I'm Erin."

"You look so young to be a doctor!"

"I'm a Ph.D.," Erin explained.

"Dr. Casey is a forensic anthropologist," Dawson said. "She consults with the Chicago Police Department, as well as other law enforcement organizations throughout the Midwest."

Maggie Gallagher couldn't quite hide her surprise. "A forensic anthropologist. That means you work with—"

"Bones," Erin supplied. "Skeletal remains. I help with identification."

"She does much more than that," Dawson said, his expression almost grim. "A good forensic anthropologist can also determine cause and manner of death. Their expert testimony has helped us convict countless murderers who would have otherwise gone free."

"My goodness." Maggie looked dutifully impressed. "Are you here with your husband, Dr. Casey?"

"I'm not married."

Maggie's brows lifted ever so slightly. "I'll be sure to tell my sons that I met you."

Three sons in the police department, Erin mused. And by the looks of things, Maggie Gallagher and the superintendent were a little more than mere acquaintances. His hand rested possessively on her back, and when Maggie glanced up at him, the two exchanged a look that was unmistakable.

He bent down to say something to her, and Erin used the interlude to make her escape. Murmuring her excuses to Dean Stanton, she drifted away, melting once more into the crowd.

She wondered if she could slip away altogether and not be noticed. She still had to go by the lab and pack her equipment for the excavation, then call Detective Gallagher...

Lost in thought about the next day's work, she jumped slightly when someone said her name. She turned, meeting Superintendent Dawson's cool gaze, and again Erin felt a vague uneasiness. As head of the Chicago Police Department, he was a very important man. She wanted to believe her disquiet was a result of his title and position, but there was something else about him, a hardness in his eyes that could have been the result of his years on the police force, but somehow Erin suspected it was not.

She thought him a cold man, perhaps even cruel, and she had a hard time picturing a woman like Maggie Gallagher being drawn to him. But then again, he *was* very attractive. In some ways, charismatic, which could make him a very dangerous man.

"I hope you don't mind my seeking you out like this," he said.

"Of course not," she lied.

"I wanted to tell you again how much I appreciate your discretion. I know Dean Stanton can be—shall we say—persuasive, and I admire the way you held your ground with him."

Erin wished she could take pleasure in Dawson's praise, but something told her he had an ulterior motive for his comments. "Discretion is part of my job," she said with a light shrug. "Just as it is with yours."

"Actually, your job is what I'd like to talk to you about." He smiled down at her, but Erin couldn't detect a single note of warmth or amusement in his eyes. "I don't like uncleared cases, but unfortunately, our files are full of Jane and John Does, many of them homicides whose perpetrators were never apprehended because the victims couldn't be identified. Your work is extremely important to CPD, Dr. Casey. Make no mistake about that."

"I appreciate that," Erin told him. "My work is very important to me, too."

"Your dedication is obvious." He hesitated, then said pensively, "I'm wondering if you might be interested in participating on a task force I'm putting together for our Missing Persons Bureau. Your input could be invaluable."

An alarm sounded inside Erin, but she tried to keep her tone and expression neutral. "I'm flattered, but my work here at the university keeps me very busy."

"I understand. But I'd like to come by your lab someday soon and discuss the project with you anyway. If you wouldn't have any objection."

His tone implied that he certainly didn't expect her to object, but she did. Apart from her heavy schedule at Hillsboro, Erin had no intention of getting involved in a police department task force. She would consult on cases within the safe confines of the university, but she would not risk questions about her background. Erin had always been very careful about keeping a low profile, even on cases that had caught the attention of the media. Now that she had returned to Chicago, it was more important than ever that she adhere to those rules. If her father were to ever find out she was here...

Who are you kidding? a little voice taunted Erin. Her presence in Chicago would make no difference to her father whatsoever. He'd gladly given away his rights to her when she was a baby, hadn't he? Relinquished all claims, legal and otherwise, in order to retain sole custody of the son he'd cherished, the only child he'd ever wanted.

She glanced up at Dawson, and it almost seemed, by the flicker in his gray eyes, that he knew what she'd been thinking. Had he somehow found out her real name, her true identity? Erin doubted it. If he knew she was from an infamous Chicago crime family, he wouldn't be asking her to sit on a police task force, would he?

"I'll have my secretary call you in a day or two," he advised. "And I must warn you, Dr. Casey, I usually don't take no for an answer."

And I must warn you, Erin thought in annoyance, *I don't take orders very well, not even from the superintendent of the Chicago Police Department.*

"DR. CASEY, isn't it? Mary Alice Stanton." The dean's wife blocked Erin's path to the front door, where she had hoped to quietly slip out unnoticed. "I'm so happy to finally meet you. Phil's been raving about your credentials ever since you accepted the position here at Hillsboro.''

Erin shook hands with the woman. ''That's nice to hear,'' she murmured, although she couldn't imagine Dean Stanton raving about anyone or anything. And after her less than sterling performance with Ed Dawson, whatever admiration Dean Stanton might have been harboring for her would have quickly evaporated.

On closer examination, the dean's wife was a little older than Erin had first thought, probably around thirty. They were contemporaries, but for the life of her, Erin couldn't think of a single thing to say to the woman. Mary Alice was beautiful, sexy and glamorous, and judging by the revealing dress she wore, she knew it. There was nothing wrong in that. Erin admired confidence. But women like Mary Alice Stanton, and like Erin's secretary, Gloria, always made her feel inadequate, and it wasn't a feeling she liked.

''I couldn't help noticing that you were having a private conversation with Superintendent Dawson,'' Mary Alice observed. ''He's a very interesting man, isn't he? And so attractive!''

''Yes, he is,'' Erin agreed, though not enthusiastically.

Mary Alice appeared not to notice. Her eyes glowed with admiration. ''He and my husband have been friends for years, and I went to college with his stepdaughter. That's how Phil and I met.''

Erin wasn't sure how she was supposed to respond to that, so she merely smiled.

Mary Alice lowered her voice intimately. ''You may have heard what happened to her.''

''The stepdaughter?''

She nodded sadly, but there was a strange glow in

her eyes, almost as if she relished retelling the story. "Her name was Ashley Dallas. She was murdered eight years ago at a college party. Not Hillsboro," she quickly added, as if to assuage any fears the information may have generated in Erin. "A man was convicted of her murder, and he's been on death row for several years. Now, however, there's a possibility he may be released."

Something akin to a premonition swept over Erin. She felt chill bumps up and down her bare arms. "Why?"

Mary Alice shrugged. "Some unfortunate legal technicality. It was discovered a few months ago that evidence was deliberately withheld from the police investigation, and the man's lawyers have pressed for a mistrial or a new trial or something. There was a real brouhaha in the papers about it a few months ago, and some of his groupies organized a protest march at police headquarters. According to the newspaper accounts, the scene got pretty violent."

"I haven't heard anything about it." Erin rarely had time for reading newspapers or even watching the news on television, which quite often made her feel hopelessly out of the loop. She supposed she was the quintessential scientist, cooped up in her lab and shut off from the rest of the world.

"I'm surprised, given the level of publicity it's received," Mary Alice said. "But then, I guess you haven't been in town all that long, and things have recently died down a bit." She looked as if she wanted to say more, but just then, Russell Quay, another anthropology professor and member of the FAHIL staff, hurried over and tapped her on the shoulder.

Mary Alice turned, automatically plastering a smile

on her lovely face. "Russell! I haven't seen you all evening. Where've you been hiding, you handsome devil, you?"

The diminutive professor beamed up at her, obviously smitten, and when Mary Alice bent to say something to him, putting her "attributes" at his eye level, Erin thought he might faint dead away.

After a moment, Mary Alice excused herself, and her admirer turned anxiously to follow her with his gaze. Behind his thick, bottlelike glasses, his eyes looked dazed and slightly guilty, like a kid who'd purloined his father's *Penthouse*.

"Dr. Quay?"

He turned, startled, as if he hadn't seen Erin standing there. His face flushed a deep, mottled red, and he muttered something under his breath, quickly whirling away to run headlong into a uniformed server carrying a heavy, silver tray of canapés. Somehow the young woman managed to keep her balance, and after a bit of two-stepping, Russell darted around her and disappeared into the crowd.

"The poor man is obviously sexually deprived," Lois Childers, an archaeology professor, commented wryly as she ambled up beside Erin. "That's the kind you have to watch out for, you know. Their frustrations sometimes manifest themselves in very disturbing ways."

"You sound as if you've had some experience," Erin remarked mildly. Lois was a tall woman, in her early forties, with handsome features and a raspy, sexy voice deepened even more so by her chain smoking. Her auburn hair was shoulder length and blunt cut in a Cleopatra style that highlighted her angular cheekbones. Tonight she wore a gold brocade suit that made her seem positively regal as she gazed upon the proceedings with airy disdain.

"I've known my share of head cases," she blithely admitted. "I'd watch out for Russell if I were you."

Erin glanced at her in surprise. "Why?"

Lois shrugged. "He thought he would be the one put in charge of FAHIL. Dean Stanton gave him every indication that he would be, then suddenly—" she snapped her fingers "—here you are."

"I didn't know," Erin said, although it was hardly a surprise. Universities were as competitive as multinational corporations. Her appointment was bound to cause some hostility. "I don't know Dr. Quay all that well, but he doesn't seem threatening."

"Well, hell," Lois said, eyeing Erin over the rim of her wineglass. "Neither do many serial killers." She paused. "I'll lay you two to one odds that the little general is still a virgin. His mommy keeps him on too tight a leash."

"His mommy?"

Lois snorted. "Didn't you know? Russell still lives with his mother. He asked me to dinner once and the old bag had to come along with us. Do you remember the mother in *Throw Momma from the Train*?" When Erin admitted she did, Lois nodded grimly. "Well, then, you've got the picture."

"You've dated Russell Quay?" Erin hadn't meant to sound so incredulous, but a more unlikely couple she couldn't imagine.

"Well, hell," Lois said. "I'm not getting any younger, and besides, in case you haven't noticed, the pickings on campus aren't exactly prime. We can't all have tall, dark, handsome detectives traipsing through our offices."

Erin froze. How had Lois known about Detective Gallagher?

Almost casually, she said, "So, who have you been talking to?"

Lois smiled mysteriously. "I have my sources."

"This is serious, Lois. If there's a leak at FAHIL—"

Lois rolled her eyes. "Oh, come on. Lighten up, Erin. A good-looking man causes talk. I saw him coming out of your office and I asked Gloria who he was. She obviously had the hots for him herself."

Gloria Maynard hadn't exactly overwhelmed Erin with her competence and trustworthiness, and now to hear that she'd been talking about a visitor to the lab, even to Lois, did not bode well for their future working relationship. Erin would have to speak to her secretary at once, warn her to be especially discreet where FAHIL was concerned.

Still, Lois was right. A good-looking man did cause talk, and Nick Gallagher was nothing if not good-looking. An image of him flashed through Erin's mind, and she felt that same flutter of nerves in her stomach that she'd experienced upon meeting him. She told herself again it wasn't attraction. She had some sort of sixth sense about the man. Some internal alarm warning her that he meant trouble.

Lois gave her a smug look. "I'll lay you ten to one odds that man doesn't live with his mother."

No, Erin thought. For all she knew, he lived with his wife. Or his lover.

That notion gave her another odd feeling, making her stomach tremble even more, and she took a sip of her wine, trying to chase away the unfamiliar sensation.

"And I can tell you without a doubt, he's no virgin," Lois declared.

Erin gave her an amused glance. "Without a doubt? You know, of course, that implies a certain knowledge of the fact."

Lois gave a sensual wince. "Don't I wish. That dark hair with those blue eyes...that body..." She shuddered. "He'd be an incredible lover."

Erin's amusement evaporated, and she became annoyed with the conversation, although she couldn't say why exactly. "Just because he's good-looking—"

"It's more than that," Lois declared. "When you get to be my age, you have a certain instinct for men. It's like a radar. You know almost immediately the ones who'll remember your birthday, the ones who'll be nice to your mother. The ones who'll be good in bed," she added with a sly smile.

"And you think Detective Gallagher would be nice to your mother?" Erin couldn't help asking.

"Honey chile, my dear ole mother would drool all over him," Lois drawled, mimicking Erin's Southern accent.

"Would he remember your birthday?"

Lois gave that a moment's consideration. "No," she said finally. "He's not the type of man who would remember a woman's birthday. But he'd sure as hell know how to make it up to her."

ERIN STEPPED OUT onto the portico of the dean's house a few minutes later, breathing a sigh of relief that she'd finally made good her escape. Then she paused as her gaze lit on a man lurking on the sidewalk across the street. He stood beneath the limbs of a giant elm, his face filtered from the streetlight, and for a moment, Erin's heart started to race. Had he followed her here?

Had he been standing there all evening, waiting for her to come out? If so, why?

An image of the skeletal remains of Case 00-03, locked tight in her lab, flashed through Erin's head, and panic bloomed inside her. Just as she turned to go back inside the house, the man stepped into the street, leaving the shadows behind, and Erin recognized him. She felt relief and anxiety all at once, and her heart continued to pound as she watched Detective Gallagher cross the street and head up the flower-lined walkway.

He'd be an incredible lover.

Erin cursed herself for lingering as long as she had over that conversation with Lois, because now she couldn't get the woman's observations concerning Detective Gallagher out of her head.

Honestly, Erin told herself irritably. Whether the man was Don Juan himself had no bearing on her dealings with him.

And I can tell you without a doubt, he's no virgin.

Brilliant, Erin thought dryly. It didn't exactly take a Nobel prize winner in genetic engineering to reach that conclusion. Anyone who had gazed into those baby blues would have deduced that much in two seconds flat, even a forensic anthropologist whose sexual exploits—and it was being extremely imaginative to use that term—were few and far between.

When he drew near her, his steps faltered for one split second before he approached her. "Dr. Casey?"

"Yes."

"I almost didn't recognize you." His gaze swept over her, taking in her loose, flowing hair and the clingy fabric of her tunic and pants. The look on his face made Erin grow almost breathless.

"H-how did you know I'd be here?" she said, wincing inwardly at the stammer.

"Your secretary told me."

Gloria again. Not only did the woman talk too much, she wasn't above selling out her boss in order to gain the favor of an attractive man.

Well, who could blame her? a little voice jeered as Erin's gaze slipped over Detective Gallagher in the dim light. He'd shed the sport coat and slacks he'd worn earlier in favor of jeans and a cotton T-shirt which melded very nicely to his muscular torso. Erin was beginning to appreciate a little more than just his bone structure, she realized. Perhaps she hadn't given enough credit in the past to toned muscles and tanned skin.

And now you sound just like Lois, that same little voice taunted her.

Well, hell, Erin thought, wrapping her shawl more tightly around her shoulders.

"Are you ready to go?" His gaze flicked over her again, as if he still wasn't quite convinced she was the woman he'd been expecting.

Erin knew she should be flattered, but for some reason she wasn't. Had her appearance been that lacking earlier?

And so what if it had? Why should she care what Detective Gallagher, or anyone else, thought of her looks? Erin had never been a vain person. There had always been so many more interesting pursuits with which to occupy her time. She didn't even like to shop. She'd ordered the outfit she had on tonight via the Internet, not having concerned herself for more than a minute with the fit, color, or fabric.

Judging by Detective Gallagher's reaction, the selection was a success, and Erin felt herself growing even more agitated the longer he stared at her.

She pushed back her hair. "I'll need to go home and change first. Then I'll have to go by the lab and pick up my equipment."

"Fine. I'll drive you."

Erin started to tell him she had her own car, but then she remembered that she'd walked the few blocks from her garage apartment to the dean's house, not wanting to be bothered with parking on the narrow street. It had still been daylight then, but now that it was dark and growing cool, she didn't relish walking home alone. She shrugged. "Thanks. I'd appreciate the ride."

They started down the marble steps together, and he took her elbow. An old-fashioned, courtly gesture that Erin suspected had been drummed into him by his mother. But for some reason, his touch seemed intimate and knowing, as if he were all too aware of Erin's reaction to him.

I've been in the lab too long, she thought almost in panic, *if my insides turn to jelly by the mere touch of an attractive man.*

But Ed Dawson's touch hadn't affected her that way, Erin reminded herself. Quite the contrary, the feel of his hand on hers had been almost repugnant, and his age had nothing to do with it. She'd always been attracted to older men, and Dawson had the same timeless appeal as Sean Connery. Yet Erin's instincts had been wary of him from the first and she didn't know why.

She wondered what Nick Gallagher thought of his mother dating the superintendent of the police department. Did that pave the way for him and his brothers to rise in the ranks?

Erin had an instinct for Nick Gallagher, too, and she didn't think he was the type of person who would ride another's coattails. He was restless, driven, almost dogmatic, she suspected, when battling for a cause he believed in. And God help anyone who got in his way.

She shivered as his grasp on her tightened almost imperceptibly when they reached the end of the walkway and he guided her toward his car. "This way."

He dropped his hand from her elbow, and Erin experienced that same sense of relief and anxiety she'd felt earlier. What was it about him that kept her so off center? She hadn't felt this way, at least not so quickly, even when she'd fallen madly in love with one of her professors her first year of college. The affair had been disastrous, naturally, because he'd been older and wiser and, she'd discovered too late, married.

A wave of shame washed over her at the memory, but Erin tried to shove it to the farthest recesses of her mind. No use crying over spilt milk, her mother had always told her.

Detective Gallagher opened the door of his car, and Erin slid inside, admiring the smell and feel of the leather seats. The sports car was an import, not one of the more expensive ones, but low-slung and fast just the same. He climbed in on the other side and started the powerful engine, glancing in the rearview mirror before pulling away from the curb.

The interior of the car was dark and close, the glow from the dash casting only the faintest of light on his features. He barely glanced at her, but seemed deeply preoccupied by his own thoughts. Was he thinking about the remains they would excavate in the morning? Was he wondering about the identity?

Was he keeping something from her? Erin wondered uneasily.

They spoke very little on the way to her place, and once he'd parked on the street near her garage apartment, Erin debated on whether she should invite him up. Better not, she decided, remembering her conversation with Lois. Best to keep their time together on a strictly business level.

"I'll just be a moment," she told him.

She opened her door, and the bright light seemed to catch them both by surprise. Their eyes met, and for the longest moment, Erin remained still, mesmerized by the intensity of his gaze. Finally he said, "I appreciate the way you rearranged your schedule."

She shrugged. "No problem. This is what I do."

He smiled faintly. "A bone detective."

The smile sent a shiver of awareness racing up her spine. "That's right."

"I hope you can work your magic for me, Dr Casey."

She lifted a brow. "Don't you mean for your friend? The county sheriff you mentioned?"

His blue gaze flickered. "Yeah. Sure. If you can identify those remains, you'll be doing us both a big favor."

"I'll identify the remains," Erin told him confidently. She climbed out of the car and glanced back at him. "But I still believe there's a lot more to this case than you've told me."

His smile vanished. "I've told you everything you need to know," he said coolly. "You do your job, Dr. Casey, and I'll do mine."

Chapter Three

You do your job, Dr. Casey, and I'll do mine.

Erin couldn't say she appreciated his attitude, but she wasn't surprised by it. She'd worked with police officers before who grudgingly enlisted her help and were all too quick to draw the line between her duties and theirs. Homicide detectives were an especially turf-conscious breed.

Changing quickly into jeans and a long-sleeve shirt, Erin packed a small overnight bag, put out plenty of food and water for her cat, Macavity, and then locked up her apartment. Detective Gallagher was leaning against his car waiting for her as she ran down the stairs. He opened his trunk and stored her bag, then they both climbed back into the car.

For a long, tense moment, neither of them said anything. His earlier rejoinder seemed to have dampened whatever camaraderie might have been forming between them. Erin saw him drum his fingertips impatiently on the steering wheel, and then hesitantly he turned to her. "Look, I'm sorry about before. What I said earlier."

She shrugged. "No problem."

"No, I was out of line and I apologize. It's just

that…'' He trailed off, lifting a hand to rub th
of his neck. "I'm under some pressure right n

"I understand, Detective Gallagher.'' Actu
was impressed that he was even willing to
It had been her experience that most police officers,
especially detectives, weren't.

He flashed her another look. "Call me Nick.''

"Then please call me Erin.''

He gave her a quick smile that almost stopped her
heart. "Nice Irish name. My grandmother would ap-
prove.''

"You're Irish, too,'' she said needlessly, but his
smile had addled her a bit. She'd never been so aware
of a man's presence before. She didn't quite know how
to handle it.

Nick didn't seem to have the same problem. He said
easily, "My father's parents were both born in Dublin.
You should hear my grandmother. Sometimes her
brogue is still so thick you can barely understand her,
especially when she gets mad. The fact that none of
her grandchildren went to Notre Dame has been a sore
spot with her for years now.''

Erin smiled, but didn't comment. According to her
mother, her paternal grandfather had also immigrated
to America from Ireland, over seventy years ago, where
he had almost immediately set about to build himself
an empire. He had been a bootlegger to start, an Irish
Al Capone, and then after the repeal of prohibition, the
family import-export business had diversified into other
illegal activities, including arms trading.

His sons—one of them being Erin's father—had followed in his footsteps, which was why Erin's mother
had struck the bargain with him that she had. If she
couldn't save both her children from his evil influence,

she could at least save one. So she took Erin—the child her father had agreed to give up—and fled Chicago, while Erin's brother remained behind.

In all these years, Erin had never heard a word from her father. When she was younger and her mother had told her about their past, she'd been too frightened to want any contact. Then, in high school, when she'd gone through a brief period of rebellion, she'd convinced herself that her father's complete absence from her life was because he didn't know where she and her mother had gone off to, nor did he know their new names. If she could just talk to him, let him know where she was, why then, of course he'd welcome her back into his life with open arms.

Her mother had figured out what Erin was up to and had warned her that any connection with her father whatsoever could be dangerous to both of them. Something in her mother's tone, the fear in her eyes had made a believer out of Erin. She hadn't been so much worried for herself as she had been for her mother. What if her father *did* decide he wanted Erin back? What would he do to her mother?

Erin had never tried to get in touch with him again, and as far as she knew, neither had her mother, although there had been times when Erin had wondered. Her mother had grown so sad during the years before she died. Melancholy and guilt-ridden, she would cry softly in her room late at night, when she thought Erin was asleep, but when Erin had tried to talk to her about it, her mother would grow very remote.

And now she was gone, and Erin would never know the deep, dark secret that had troubled her mother's last years.

She sensed Nick watching her, and she turned, meeting his eyes in the dim light. His gaze was dark, intense, curious. He was wondering about her. Speculating about what made her tick. Erin had the same curiosity about him.

"You're wondering why someone would decide to become a bone detective," she said.

His brows lifted slightly before he returned his gaze to the road. "I think I get why you're so good at what you do. You have ESP."

In truth, he wasn't far off the mark. Erin's ability to read bones did at times border on the uncanny, but she'd always been good at putting together puzzles. One of her strongest virtues was patience, another diligence. She would labor over remains long after everyone else was either satisfied with the conclusions or had given up.

"I love what I do. There's nothing supernatural about it," she told him.

He glanced at her again. "Which brings me back to my original question. Why did you become a forensic anthropologist?"

"The short answer?" Erin shrugged. "I'd always been interested in archaeology, and after the Indiana Jones movies came out, I decided, like a few thousand other students, that was what I wanted to do. Travel the world looking for rare, priceless artifacts that could either save or destroy mankind."

The look he gave her was surprised. "You don't strike me as the romantic type."

"Some people might take that as an insult," she said dryly. "But since it's the truth, I won't allow myself to be too offended."

He grinned suddenly, the smile igniting a spark in

his eyes that was very, very attractive. "You're not at all what I expected."

"No?" Her tone remained light, in spite of her racing pulse. "Let me guess. You were expecting a cross between Quincy and Jessica Fletcher. Am I right?"

"You're perceptive," he said. "I'll give you that."

"You don't exactly fit my image of a homicide detective, either," she told him. "Where's your rumpled trench coat?"

The amusement faded from his expression. "Unfortunately, in real life, we're not like Columbo. We don't always get our man. Some of them tend to slip through the legal cracks. Even cold-blooded murderers."

Something in his voice, an edge of suppressed rage, made Erin shiver. She stared at his profile for a moment, wondering why the remains discovered yesterday were so important to him. He could pretend all he wanted that he was doing a favor for a friend by enlisting her help, but Erin knew better. There was a lot more to this case than Nick Gallagher was willing to tell her, and she wondered uneasily if she was getting into something she might wish she hadn't.

"So you wanted to be Indiana Jones," he said after a moment, but the lightness had completely vanished from his tone and his expression. "Why the switch to anthropology?"

"Archaeology is a subdiscipline of anthropology. I didn't really switch, I just changed my focus." She smiled a little. "Actually, I discovered that digging trenches, millimeter by millimeter, in search of a pottery shard wasn't quite as glamorous as Harrison Ford had led me to believe, though it can be fascinating at times. I became more interested in physical anthropology, and one of my professors, who was also a forensic anthropologist, told my class a story once about a woman's daughter who had been missing for more than twenty years. When the child's remains were finally discovered and identified, the woman wrote Dr. Ellis a long letter, thanking him for bringing her daughter back home to her. For the first time in more than twenty years, the woman finally had peace. She no longer searched faces in malls or on crowded streets, wondering if one of them might be her daughter's." Erin paused. "I knew from that moment on, that's what I wanted to do, too."

"You're lucky then. Some people never figure out what it is they want in life."

She looked at him in surprise. "You don't like being a detective?"

He shrugged. "I guess I never gave it much thought. It was expected of me. I come from a long line of cops. My father, my grandfather. Both my brothers." He shrugged again. "It's in my genes, I guess."

Erin didn't like to think about genes, about what propensities could be handed down from one generation to the next. Intellectually, she knew that environment played a huge part in the development of personality traits, and she thanked her mother for giving her a safe, sheltered childhood away from her father's influence.

But she knew, too, that more and more was being discovered about heredity all the time, and that some experts now believed the tendency toward violent and criminal behavior could be passed on to a child from his or her parents. Whether Erin liked it or not, she also carried her father's genes inside her, and she knew that that knowledge had played no insignificant role in her decision to become a forensic anthropologist. By giving back to society, she could somehow counteract the darkness that might be lurking inside her.

But that wasn't a story for a police detective. She suspected Nick Gallagher wasn't a man who trusted easily, and if they were going to work together on this case, it was essential they at least have faith in each other's abilities.

He pulled into a space in the faculty parking lot near the George Augustine Building of Natural Sciences. The FAHIL lab and offices were in a new wing, a little over a year old, which jutted out from the original structure, giving it an ungainly look that was at odds with the quaint setting of the campus.

Nick and Erin got out of the car and walked up the steps to the front entrance. Erin removed her keys from her briefcase, but the door was unlocked. She glanced up at Nick, who was scowling.

"I thought you said this place was always kept locked."

"The lab is, unless I'm inside working. But the cleaning crew has to have access to the main building, plus, the faculty offices are in here, as well as some classrooms."

She led him down the deserted corridor, their footsteps echoing hollowly against the tile floor. The hallways in the original portion of the building were like a maze, and it had taken Erin several days to get her bearings when she first came here. She headed unfailingly now, however, to the door that would grant them access to the new wing.

It was unlocked, too, and before Erin could step inside, Nick moved in front of her.

Erin said quickly. "Someone's probably working late. One of the staff—"

He silenced her with a look as he glided, ghostlike, along the dim corridor. Erin, shivering by this time, didn't know what else to do but follow. The hair at the back of her neck rose as they crept along the hallway, Nick pausing now and then to check locked doors.

"How can we get to the lab from here?" he asked softly.

"We can't. We have to take the elevator up to the third floor, where the FAHIL offices are located. There's another elevator there that leads straight to the basement."

He gave her a sharp look. "There's no outside door to the lab?"

"There's an emergency exit that's kept locked," she said. "It can be opened from the inside, and that's where deliveries are handled. But someone has to be in the lab to disengage the lock."

"There's an alarm on the door, I assume."

"Of course. The other entrance to the lab is from the hallway."

"Who has a key?"

"I told you. Only the FAHIL staff."

"What about Gloria Maynard?"

"Gloria?" For some reason, the fact that he remembered her secretary's name annoyed Erin. So he hadn't been quite as immune to the woman's charms as he'd let on. "She doesn't have a key to the lab, but I've let her use mine from time to time."

He gave her a look, but Erin merely shrugged. "I've occasionally sent her down there to fetch something I needed for a class or consultation," she explained. "She doesn't particularly like going down there, so it doesn't happen all that often."

They were at the elevators now, and Erin pressed the

button. As the car descended toward them, Nick pulled her back, shielding her with his body as the doors slid open.

"Look, I don't think there's anything to worry about," she said as she moved around him and entered the elevator. "Obviously, someone is still here working."

Nick didn't say anything as he stepped into the elevator beside her. But his profile was rigidly set as he faced forward, and she wondered suddenly if he had a gun underneath his jacket.

Erin pushed the button for the third floor and the doors slid closed. The car gave a little lurch, scrambling her stomach, then slowly ascended.

When they got off on the third floor, Erin glanced around, uneasy in spite of herself. She'd never before noticed how dark the hallway was. There was one light at the far end, near the stairwell, but from the elevator down to her office, the corridor was dim and shadowy.

She'd worked late a lot of nights and never minded the poor lighting before. So why now, with a rugged police detective by her side, did gooseflesh prickle along her arms and neck as she and Nick walked down the hallway to her office?

Gloria's office was directly past the elevator, in an open lobby area that serviced the entire FAHIL staff. Erin's office was at the far end of the hallway, and as they approached her door, she became more and more apprehensive. What if her office had been broken into? What if sensitive files had been taken, cases compromised?

But when she tried her door, it was locked tight, and she let out a breath of relief. Inserting the key, she opened the door and reached inside to turn on the light, her gaze automatically scanning the interior.

Nothing was amiss. Her file cabinets were all secured, as were her desk drawers. She'd cleaned off the surface of her desk earlier, years of practice making her meticulous in putting away her work before she left for the day.

"Everything seems okay in here," Nick said, gazing around. He turned back around to face her. "Let's go have a look in the lab."

She nodded. "I have to get my equipment together anyway, but I'm sure we'll find it locked up tight, just like my office."

He cut her another look, one that said, so far, he wasn't all that impressed with Hillsboro's security.

Erin frowned, feeling defensive but trying to subdue it. No use getting off on more of an adversarial footing with him than she already had. Still, if there was one area of her life where she felt secure, it was her work. She knew what she was doing, and she didn't much care for someone challenging her competence.

After locking her office, they got in the service elevator, which took them directly to the basement level. The hallway there was dim and shadowy, too, and as Erin disengaged the alarm and motion detectors, she silently vowed to have maintenance install better lighting as soon as possible.

She unlocked the door to the lab, and both she and Nick walked inside. Hesitating for one split second before turning on the lights, she gave him time to absorb the ambiance of the lab in darkness. The safety lights did little more than cast shadows and highlight the shelves of skulls, and Erin had heard Gloria Maynard declare more than once that you would not catch her dead in this place after dark. Erin always got a silent chuckle out of the irony.

She glanced up at Nick, sensing more than seeing his tension in the murky light. She heard him mutter something beneath his breath, and she said quite casually, "Excuse me?"

"Unless you want to tell ghost stories, you can turn on the light now."

Erin flipped the switch, giving him an amused glance. "Not spooked, are you, detective?"

He flinched slightly when the overhead lights came on, then cut her a dry look. "Let me guess. Halloween is your favorite holiday. What do you do—decorate the skulls?"

Erin's amusement vanished. "I wouldn't do that," she said simply. "I respect the remains that I work on, and I never lose sight of the fact that they were once someone's brother or daughter or mother."

Nick's gaze on her was intense. He seemed to understand exactly what she meant, and for the longest moment, he remained silent. Then he glanced away and said in a subdued tone, "I think I've come to the right place."

NICK EXAMINED the outside door. "This can only be opened from in here, you say?"

Erin walked over to join him. "Yes. It was originally intended for an emergency exit, but we also use it for deliveries. It opens up into an alley."

"How about if I go out this way and have a look around?"

Erin shrugged. "Sure. You may as well bring your car around, and we can load the equipment from here." She entered the code, then gave him the all-clear signal.

He shoved open the heavy door almost reluctantly, glancing back as it closed between them. He didn't like leaving her inside the lab alone, even though he knew she was comfortable with her surroundings and probably safer inside those walls than most any other place in Chicago. Still, he'd seen another side of Dr. Erin Casey tonight, and it was hard to dispel the image of all that flowing hair, that clingy outfit. It was hard to think of her as anything other than a woman now.

He shook his head, as if to clear his mind, and climbed the steps to street level. The alley was a dead end, bordered on one side by the FAHIL building and on the other by an eight-foot concrete wall. There was only one way in and one way out, and depending on the size of the delivery vehicle, he could imagine a driver having a hard time reversing all the way to the end.

The lab, by the very nature of the work performed there, was a little creepy, and Nick had been unsettled by the thought of bringing the skeletal remains of someone he'd known—someone he'd loved—here to be coldly and clinically examined by a stranger.

Erin had set his mind to rest. She was the right person for the job. Passionate, discreet, thoroughly professional, there was nothing about her with which he could quarrel. He hoped a judge and jury would feel the same way, because depending on her findings, Nick would try his damnedest to build an ironclad case against Daniel O'Roarke for the murder of Sean Gallagher, Nick's father.

Eight years ago, O'Roarke had been arrested for the brutal slaying of Ashley Dallas, the beautiful, young stepdaughter of Police Superintendent Ed Dawson, and the woman Nick's younger brother, Tony, had been in

love with. Nick's father had been the lead detective on
the case, assigned by Dawson himself because Sean
Gallagher had been the best on the force. Sean had
made the arrest, then a few weeks later, he disappeared.
His body was never found, but there'd never been any
doubt in Nick's mind that Daniel O'Roarke, out on bail
awaiting trial, had killed Sean for revenge.

The MO was typical of the O'Roarkes, who had
been mortal enemies of the Gallaghers ever since William Gallagher, Nick's grandfather, and James
O'Roarke had emigrated from Ireland together over
seventy years ago. William had become a cop, James
a criminal, but they'd had one thing in common—their
love for Nick's grandmother, Colleen. She'd been engaged to James, but had married William when she'd
learned of James's illicit activities. The rivalry between
the two men had become even more fierce after that,
and the bitterness had been passed down through the
generations.

The O'Roarkes, with their shady alliances and illegal
dealings, were an anathema to everything the Gallaghers stood for, and after Sean disappeared, Nick had
begun his own personal crusade against them.

Daniel O'Roarke had eventually been convicted of
Ashley Dallas's murder and given the death penalty.
Over the years, an army of powerful lawyers, hired by
Daniel's father, Richard, had tried one appeal after another. Nothing had worked until a few months ago,
when new information had come to light which suggested that both Sean Gallagher and Ed Dawson had
suppressed evidence in the case that might have, if not
cleared Daniel, at least created reasonable doubt.

Armed with this potentially explosive information,
the O'Roarke attorneys had petitioned the court to

overturn Daniel's conviction, in which case, Daniel would walk out of prison a free man. And because of the O'Roarkes' money and influence, not to mention their willingness to use extortion when necessary, Daniel's freedom appeared to not only be a possibility but a probability.

For weeks now Nick had had to live with the image of his father's murderer plastered across the news broadcasts. He'd had to listen to the impassioned pleas of starlets and zealots, begging the courts to set Daniel O'Roarke free. O'Roarke even had a web site in his honor, created and maintained by one of his most ardent admirers, a young woman who claimed she and O'Roarke were in love.

Not once did any of these people stop to consider the victims' families, Nick thought bitterly. Not once did they stop to think what it would be like to have your father's murderer roaming free, willing and able to kill again. Not once did they stop to contemplate that even if information had been withheld from the official police report, the evidence against O'Roarke had still been sufficiently overwhelming to convince a jury of his guilt.

Never before had Nick felt so enraged by the judicial system, nor so helpless. But then, like divine intervention, Roy Glass, the sheriff in Webber County, Wisconsin, had called and told him about the discovery of a skeleton in the woods near the fishing cabin from which Nick's father had disappeared. If the remains turned out to be Sean's and if Nick could prove his father had been murdered, then he would begin very systematically to build another case against Daniel O'Roarke.

After eight long years of waiting, there would finally be justice for Sean Gallagher. And for Nick.

UNLIKE VISITORS to the lab, Erin was never frightened by her surroundings. She usually became so absorbed in her work that she never stopped to think about the potential "chill" factor, but ever since her conversation with Nick earlier that day, she'd felt an unprecedented sense of unease she couldn't seem to shake.

Tonight, after finding the building unlocked, the feeling had deepened, and as Erin stood in the deserted lab, a shiver skimmed along her arms.

Probably served her right, she decided, for trying to scare poor Detective Gallagher earlier. Not that he appeared to be a man who frightened easily, but he had been uncomfortable with the lights off and he hadn't tried to pretend otherwise. Erin liked that about him. He didn't exhibit any of the forced machismo she'd seen so often in police officers. But then, he didn't have to. He exuded an innate strength and sense of self that needed no false bolstering. He was one of the most interesting men she'd ever met.

Telling herself she didn't have time to stand around all night analyzing Detective Gallagher's manly qualities, she set about gathering up the equipment she would need for the excavation, including her Marshalltown trowel.

Busy with her work, the noise that came from somewhere behind her barely registered at first, but then, like a midday shadow, the realization that she wasn't alone came creeping over her, and the hair on the back of her neck rose in warning.

She didn't immediately turn, but stood for a moment, trying to analyze the noise—what it had been, where it had come from. The walls and doors in the lab where thick, but every once in a while, when everything was dead silent, like now, noises from the outside would filter in. Erin could sometimes even hear the faint, telltale clang of the elevator as it descended from the third floor.

Initially, she'd chalked those sounds up to imagination, but then almost inevitably someone would appear at the lab door—one of the staff, Gloria, a visitor. Erin had gotten used to this early warning system, and had decided that she had either been blessed with exceptional hearing, which she'd never appreciated before, or the vents in the lab were situated in such a way as to magnify sound from the hallway. If the latter was the case, no one else seemed to notice, but that was probably because she was the one most often alone in the lab—

The noise sounded again, and Erin whirled, not certain what she expected to see. Case 00-03 lay on her worktable, silent and waiting. The skulls on her shelves grinned down at her, almost comforting in their mute surveillance. The door to the X-ray room was shut tight. It wasn't anything in the lab causing her alarm. What she heard was the unmistakable clang of the elevator. Sometime after she and Nick had entered the lab, someone had summoned it back to the third floor and was now descending toward her.

It had to be a staff member because no one else had a key to the lab. That knowledge should have made Erin feel better, but somehow it didn't. As far as she knew, no one else ever worked this late. Moreover, she required prior notification if anyone did want to use the lab, so whoever was on his or her way to the basement was unauthorized to do so.

Erin's first thought was to wait right where she was and catch the perpetrator red-handed, but then, as it had several times already that day, Nick's warning came back to her. *In case you haven't thought about it before, you've got a murder victim lying in your lab downstairs. Someone out there is going to be awfully unhappy when you ID her.*

As Erin stared at the door, it hit her suddenly that the lock on the lab door was still disengaged, and that she had turned off the alarm near the elevator, which triggered the motion detectors in both the hallway and the lab. If someone other than FAHIL personnel was in the elevator, then she could be in real danger.

Trowel still grasped in her hand, she flew across the room to the door, turning the heavy bolt as she pressed her face to the square of Plexiglas set in the metal. She couldn't see the elevator from the window, but she could no longer hear the clanging from the vents, so she assumed the car had reached the basement. Someone had gotten out and might even now be lurking in the gloomy hallway, waiting for Erin to open the door—

A face appeared on the other side of the glass, and Erin's heart leaped to her throat. She screamed and jumped back, and from the other side of the door came a faint, answering yelp as the face instantly disappeared.

Chapter Four

"You might have warned me you were sending him down to the lab," Erin grumbled a few minutes later as she and Nick, equipment stored in the trunk of his car, headed north on Lake Shore Drive. The lights along the lake glowed like a string of incandescent pearls, and a strong, easterly wind blew clouds across the moon, trimming the pale edges with a dark, wispy lace. The night was cool and mild, with only a hint of the rainstorm winging its way in from the Atlantic.

Erin turned her gaze back to Nick, her tone accusing. "I nearly had a heart attack when I saw Ralph's face pressed up against that glass."

Nick flashed her a grin. "You didn't get spooked in your own lab, did you, Dr. Casey?"

"Okay," she acquiesced after a moment's irritation. "Maybe I deserved that. But what about poor Ralph? In case you didn't notice, he isn't in the best of health."

The security guard at the FAHIL facilities was at least sixty pounds overweight, with a propensity for scarfing down candy bars and soft drinks while on duty. Erin suspected the caffeine in the sodas and chocolate was most often the only thing keeping him awake at night. She'd caught him napping one night in Gloria's office, head thrown back against the chair, feet propped on the desk, snoring with gusto as Erin slammed shut a file drawer. It hadn't seemed to faze him.

He was a nice man and she knew he needed the job, so she hadn't had the heart to do more than shake him awake and send him on his rounds. Besides, with the alarm system in place, a security guard had almost seemed like overkill to her. Now, she realized how vulnerable she was while working in the lab. With the motion detectors turned off, if someone did manage to manipulate the elevator from the third floor—

Erin shuddered, vowing to be more diligent about keeping the lab door locked when she worked alone at night. And she would also speak to Ralph, if the poor man didn't quit after tonight.

As if reading her mind, Nick shot her a glance, his amusement vanishing. "Out of shape or not, he's a security guard. He has a responsibility to ensure the safety of the premises, and that means finding and securing unlocked doors."

Erin winced inwardly, imagining the riot act Nick had likely read the unsuspecting guard before he'd been sent down to check on her. Ralph wasn't exactly the sharpest needle in the sewing box, as her mother used to say, and Erin hated to think of his feelings being hurt, even if he had been in the wrong. He meant well, she was sure.

"No harm done," she said briskly. "You and Ralph both checked the building and nothing was amiss, so there's no cause for concern."

The grim set of his profile in the dash lights seemed to disagree. Erin sighed. "Detective Gallagher...

Nick...I know it's your job to worry about security, but let me assure you there's never been an incident at FAHIL.''

He cut her another glance. ''The lab was only completed a year or so ago, by an anonymous donor as I understand it, and you've only been on board a little more than two months. Not exactly a tested track record.''

She lifted her chin in defense. ''That's true. But I trained and worked at one of the most prestigious labs in the country before accepting the position at Hillsboro. I know what I'm doing.''

Something in her tone must have gotten through to him, for the glance he gave her now was slightly apologetic. ''I don't doubt you know your stuff, but I know mine, too. Maybe I am being a little overcautious about security, but I'd rather be safe than sorry. Wouldn't you?''

Instead of responding to his question, she eyed him for a moment, wondering about the case he'd asked her to consult on. They entered the freeway, merging with the still-heavy traffic flowing out of town.

''These remains you've found,'' she began.

''I didn't personally find them,'' he said in a strangely tense voice.

''Okay. The remains that were found by a hunter.'' Erin paused. ''I still get the distinct impression you're not telling me everything you know about them.''

Nick shot a glance in the rearview. ''You've said that before.''

''And you've never given me a satisfactory answer. I'd like to know what I'm getting into.''

To her amazement, he slowed the car, then pulled onto the shoulder and stopped. For a moment, he sat staring straight ahead, seemingly oblivious to the blur of cars whizzing past them, causing the sports car to shimmy.

Finally he turned to her and said, "You're right. I'm not telling you everything I know about this case." Before she could protest, he added in a voice dark with foreboding, "And I'm not going to."

"But if you know something that could help me make the identification, surely—"

He stopped her again. "I need your findings to be completely unbiased."

Erin drew herself up, staring him straight in the eye. "My findings are always unbiased."

In the light from the dash, she could see something glimmer in his electric-blue gaze. "We wouldn't be making this trip if I thought otherwise. But for reasons I won't go into right now, it's crucial that your examination of these remains be impeccable. There can't be even a hint of compromise."

His meaning hit Erin all of a sudden. "You're trying to build a case against someone," she said slowly. "Someone important."

"That's not for you to worry about."

Their gazes held for a long moment, and something quick and hot passed between them. Then Nick glanced away, almost reluctantly it seemed to Erin.

"You may as well sit back and relax," he advised, putting the car into gear. "We've got a long drive ahead of us."

As he nosed the car back onto the freeway, Erin laid her head against the back of the seat and closed her eyes. But she was far from relaxed. She was too aware of the man sitting beside her, so close she could reach out and touch him if she wanted to. And to Erin's amazement, she did want to. Very much. She couldn't remember the last time she'd had a date, much less been kissed by a man she was almost desperately attracted to.

Maybe she never had been, she mused, opening her eyes and giving Nick Gallagher a sidelong glance. And if that was the case, it was Erin's opinion that it was high time she was.

THE STORM rolled in overnight, and by dawn, the sky was heavy with clouds. The rain hadn't come yet, and if the weather reports could be believed—and Nick prayed they could be—they still had several hours before the downpour.

He and Erin had spent the night in a motel several miles north of Milwaukee—in separate rooms—but the paper-thin walls hadn't allowed for much privacy. Nick had lain in bed, listening to the shower running next door, and in spite of his preoccupation with what lay ahead of them, he couldn't help imagining Erin standing beneath the steamy water, her glorious hair wet and heavy against her back.

He'd imagined himself lifting the damp strands to kiss her shoulder, to nuzzle her neck and flick his tongue against her ear. He'd pictured himself picking up her slight body, carrying her off to bed, making love to a woman he found both enigmatic and desirable.

The erotic images had surprised him as much as they'd excited him, and Nick had quickly turned off the lamp and settled himself under the covers, forcing his thoughts to turn elsewhere. But then, just as he was drifting off to sleep, he'd heard the faint squeak of the bedsprings in her room as she climbed into bed, and her voice coming so faintly through the wall it almost seemed like a dream. "Good night, Nick."

The sound of her Southern drawl, soft and intimate, had tightened his midsection, had made him realize how long it had been since he'd spent the night with a woman. He'd thought about Erin as he closed his eyes in the darkness, and when he finally fell asleep, he'd dreamed about her.

"Nick?"

Her voice was such an extension of his thoughts that for a moment, he didn't respond. They were in the car again, and she reached over to lightly touch his arm. His skin instantly reacted.

He glanced at her sitting beside him and decided that she looked a lot more rested than he felt. Obviously, she hadn't been plagued half the night by the same erotic fantasies he'd had.

She was wearing jeans, heavy work boots, and a flannel shirt over a white T-shirt. Her hair was pulled back and braided, her face scrubbed clean and anxious.

"How long do you think we have before the storm hits?" she asked him.

"Not long enough," he muttered, wishing they'd taken the time for a cup of coffee anyway.

He swung the car off the main highway onto a dirt road that was so overhung with trees, it almost seemed as if they were driving through a cave. His headlights were on, and a ground mist swirled in the beams, like smoke curling from a chimney.

After several bumpy miles, Nick finally pulled behind two police cruisers and parked at the edge of the road. "There's a cabin back in the woods," he told her. "That's where we're meeting the sheriff."

"Whose cabin is it?"

Nick hesitated, wondering if he should tell her the truth, then he shrugged. ''I know the owners. They won't mind if we use it as our base camp.''

They got out and retrieved the equipment from the trunk, then, Nick in the lead, they followed a footpath that led them through the trees.

The thick woods were hushed, heavy with a waiting stillness that somehow seemed ominous. Nick told himself it was the approaching storm that made him so uneasy, but he knew the disquiet wouldn't leave him until the bones had been excavated, identified and given a proper burial.

Until—if his father finally had been found—Nick and his family were given the chance they'd never had before to say goodbye. Daniel O'Roarke had taken that from them.

He glanced back at Erin, and she gave him a calm, reassuring look, as if she'd somehow read his thoughts. As if she really did have second sight.

The sheriff and a deputy were waiting for them on the porch of the fishing cabin that belonged to Nick's family—the same cabin from which Nick's father had disappeared eight years ago.

When Sean had first gone missing, Nick had come up here often, staying in the cabin at night where his father had stayed so many nights before him, and then tramping the woods by daylight, looking for a sign, any trace, that would lead him to his father—or to his father's body.

In time, Nick's visits had dwindled, but he'd never given up the hunt altogether. His lonely sojourns had gotten him acquainted with the county sheriff in the area, and over the years, the two of them had become friends. Roy Glass, a middle-aged man with a thickening waistline and a sparkle of good humor in his brown eyes, had often walked the woods with Nick, and when the bones had been found earlier in the week, he'd called Nick within the hour, knowing how significant the discovery could be.

Dressed in khaki uniforms with dark-brown jackets, Roy and his deputy were smoking cigarettes, drinking coffee from white foam cups, and talking quietly as Nick and Erin came out of the woods. The conversation withered as they approached the porch.

Roy lazily stubbed out his cigarette and came down the wooden steps to meet them. "Nick."

"Roy, I'd like you to meet Dr. Erin Casey. She's the forensic anthropologist I told you about. Dr. Casey, this is Roy Glass. He's the county sheriff in these parts."

He touched the brim of his hat and nodded to Erin. "Ma'am."

"Pleased to meet you, Sheriff Glass."

"Call me Roy. We don't stand on formalities around here."

"And I'm Erin," she said, shaking his hand.

He turned back to the porch. "That's Clive Avery," he said, indicating the deputy. Avery nodded curtly at the introduction, then turned away, scanning the sky with a wary eye. Tall and muscular, he was very good-looking with pale-blond hair, brilliant green eyes, and sensuous lips that would have been called pouty on a woman. A weak jaw kept him from being handsome.

Erin couldn't say why, but she disliked Avery almost at once. Perhaps it was his instant dismissal of her, his gaze having touched her only briefly before moving away, uninterested. But Erin suspected it had more to do with the man's reaction to Nick. Every time Nick spoke, the deputy's expression hardened almost imperceptibly, as if he were nursing a deep resentment. And maybe that wasn't so hard to figure. Nick was a big-city cop, coming out here to trespass on Avery's turf. In Nick's presence, Clive Avery wasn't such a big fish anymore.

But as if to reassert his status, he took the lead as the four of them tramped through the woods, handing off branches to each other as they descended gradually into a small gully. The trees and brush thickened and the low-hanging limbs snagged Erin's hair, pulling it loose from its braid.

The woods smelled of damp earth and decaying vegetation, a richly verdant scent that Erin found almost pleasant. Ahead of her, Nick swatted an insect on the back of his neck, then paused to hold back another limb while she caught up with him.

Their gazes met briefly in the gloom, and Erin sensed a new intensity about him, a nervous energy that seemed to radiate from every pore of his body. She thought about what he'd told her last night, that he didn't want her bringing a bias to this case. He was not only being cautious, but methodical. Beneath the glimmer of anger she'd seen in his eyes, beneath the nervous energy, there was a cool, calculating mind that would leave no stone unturned while building a case. Erin shivered, thinking unaccountably that she would not want to be the subject of one of his investigations.

The uneasy feeling that had harried her ever since Nick's first visit to the lab descended over her again, and suddenly the woods seemed dank and oppressive, the scent of rotting leaves no longer pleasant but symbolic. Fighting a sense of dread, Erin trudged on, wondering what secrets lay hidden among the trees.

After about ten minutes or so, they entered a small glen, an almost circular clearing surrounded by a thicket of brambles and underbrush. Here, another deputy was on duty, and he jumped to his feet when he heard them coming, the look of alarm slow to leave his features even as his mind identified the source of the noise as human—and alive.

Evidently, he'd been on guard duty all night, because Avery made a crack about a call the younger deputy had placed to the station just after midnight, and the man's face turned bright red.

"Someone was out there," he insisted, nodding vaguely toward the woods. "I swear it."

"Yeah," Avery agreed. "Someone who walks on four legs and has antlers."

Pleased by his own joke, he laughed out loud, but Nick said sharply over his merriment, "How do you know it was a deer he heard?"

Avery stopped laughing and glared at Nick. "Because I'm the one who had to haul my butt out of bed and come out here last night to baby-sit when Jamie freaked and called the station. I saw the tracks. It was a deer." His tone lowered and his gaze on Nick darkened.

Roy Glass clapped Jamie on the shoulder and smiled. "There's a salt lick around here somewhere. Chances are it was a deer, but you did the right thing, son," he said to the embarrassed deputy, who shrugged good-naturedly. But Jamie's baby face remained flamingo pink. "Better to be safe than sorry," Roy added.

Which was exactly what Nick had told her, Erin thought, glancing up at him. He was staring at Avery, and judging by Nick's expression, he didn't like the deputy any more than she did. The tension between the two men was almost palpable, and Erin, glancing at the sky, thought to herself that there were two storms brewing around her.

For the first time since they'd left the cabin, she spoke up. "We should get started. The rain may not hold off for much longer."

Her voice seemed to momentarily break the strain in the tiny glen, and the men gathered around her, watching in fascination as she unpacked her equipment. But their interest soon turned to wariness—and even downright horror on Jamie's part—as Erin began to dole out the assignments.

NICK WATCHED Erin work, preferring to concentrate on her efficiency rather than on the significance of her task. Because if he let himself dwell too long on the possibility that the skeletal remains were, in fact, his father, that Sean had been brutally murdered and then dumped here to—

For a moment, Erin disappeared and Nick saw nothing but a red haze, a blinding fury that threatened to engulf him. Then, almost as if he were still alive in that ravine, his father's voice spun through Nick's mind. "You've got to find a way to control that temper, son. Because if you don't, it'll end up controlling you."

The lecture had come after a high school basketball game during which Nick had gotten into a fistfight with one of the opposing players, and both of them had been ejected from the game. Nick's team had lost, and Sean had made Nick ride home with him after the game.

Nick had still been fighting mad and had planned on finishing the job he'd started, but Sean had gotten wind of the plans and interceded. Rather than doling out the stiff punishment Nick had expected, his father had instead talked about the feud between their family and the O'Roarkes.

"Do you understand what separates us from people like them?" his father had asked him.

Nick shrugged, more interested in revenge for having lost the game than with the life lesson his father was trying to teach him.

Sean gave him a long, probing stare. "What sets the Gallaghers apart is our fairness, our sense of right and wrong. Our willingness to control our emotions and our temper in order to do the right thing. Sometimes that means being man enough to walk away from a fight. If you don't learn how to do that, then you'll be no better than the worst of the O'Roarkes."

His father's words drifted away, and Nick was left with the uncomfortable feeling that he hadn't learned his lesson that day, not the way he should have. He still had a hard time controlling his temper and his emotions, especially where the O'Roarkes were concerned. He'd grown up believing they were his mortal enemies, had become even more convinced after his father's disappearance, and in spite of Sean's warning, Nick knew there was very little he wouldn't do to bring them down.

He glanced down now at the bones, still partially buried in their shallow grave, and a wave of sadness washed over him. How would he tell his brothers about this, his sister, Fiona? She'd been through a lot in the past few months and was only now putting her life back together after a disastrous relationship with a man who had almost destroyed her. Could she handle the discovery of their father's body?

Nick thought of his younger brother, Tony, and how

the news would affect him. He'd be okay, now that he had Eve. She was a good woman and she grounded Tony, pulled him back from that dark edge he'd always seemed so drawn to.

No need to worry about John, either. The eldest Gallagher brother had never missed their father the way the rest of them had. John had even hinted once that there might not be anything sinister in Sean's disappearance, that he might have just up and walked out on his family. Nick had never been able to forgive his brother for that, even though he knew the rift between them continued to hurt their mother.

Maggie Gallagher was the one Nick worried about now. His parents had had a stormy marriage, but Nick had never doubted that his mother loved his father deeply. She'd never remarried. Since Sean's disappearance, she'd never even so much as dated another man. That said something about their relationship, didn't it? As far as Nick was concerned, it said everything.

Forcing his thoughts back to the present, he watched Erin as she staked a rectangular area around the skeleton, working in a grid pattern that reminded him of a scene in an Indiana Jones movie. He thought about her admission that the popular movies had inspired her present career, but this was not fiction. It didn't get much more real than this.

"I'm establishing my coordinates," she told him softly, as if he had asked her a question. But the sound of her soft drawl was instantly calming, and Nick had the uncanny feeling that she had again somehow picked up on his thoughts.

Jamie Duncan, the younger deputy, was photographing the area, using the special camera that Erin had loaned him to snap dozens of shots from every conceivable angle.

Erin had put Nick and Roy Glass on the sifter, which would screen all the dirt taken from around the bones, and Clive Avery had been given the unenviable task of carrying away the mounds of sifted dirt bucket by bucket. He was not a happy camper, Nick noted in amusement. But even at that, he didn't have the most difficult job. Erin did all the digging herself, kneeling tirelessly for what seemed like hours on end, painstakingly clearing away the soil from the skeleton with her trowel, sometimes even with a teaspoon. Her patience was amazing, and her reverence for her work was appreciated in a way she couldn't know.

The storm clouds continued to build all morning, and from the look of the sky—a mass of undulating gray—rain was already falling in isolated spots around the county.

Erin seemed oblivious to the threat. Absorbed in her work, she hardly looked up. Finally, after several hours of digging, she straightened and stretched her back. Glancing around the site, she said, "Where's Avery?"

"He went back to the cabin to get sandwiches and drinks," Roy Glass told her. He got up stiffly from his position and snapped his back. "It's nearly lunchtime, in case you hadn't noticed."

Erin looked surprised. "Is it that late already?"

Nick came up beside her, but he avoided looking down at the skeleton. "Are you always like this?"

"Like what?"

"So...oblivious."

She smiled. "I can be. Sorry."

"Don't apologize. You're doing exactly what I need you to do."

She nodded briefly. "Hardest part is behind us. I guess we could all use a break." She glanced up at Nick. "There wouldn't happen to be a washroom in the cabin, would there? I could use a little freshening up," she said delicately.

"I'll walk back with you."

"No need. I can find my way. I have a perfectly good sense of direction."

"If Clive's still at the cabin, have him wait and walk back with you," Roy suggested, massaging his lower back.

Erin didn't respond, but the look she flashed Nick clearly said that Clive Avery was the last person she'd want to walk back with her.

That knowledge buoyed Nick's spirits in a way he knew it shouldn't have.

WHEN ERIN came out of the woods, Avery was standing on the cabin porch, talking into a cellular phone. The moment he saw Erin, he quickly snapped the unit shut and shoved it into his jacket pocket.

"Just checking in with the station," he muttered as Erin mounted the steps. "We're getting a lot of rain around the county. Lucky it's held off here as long as it has."

"Yes, it is," she agreed, although she suspected he hadn't been talking to the station at all. Erin was not just good at reading bones. She could read people. There was an air of deviousness about Clive Avery that put her on guard.

"First door to your left," he said, when she started across the porch. "You can't miss it."

She glanced back, catching his stare. He smiled, but

his eyes were cold and calculating, more than a little malicious.

Too bad such amazing good looks had to be wasted on someone with an ugly soul, she decided. And for some reason, that made her think of Ed Dawson, the superintendent of the Chicago Police Department. She found herself shivering as she went inside the cabin.

Erin had hoped Avery would already have headed back to the site before she came out of the bathroom, but no such luck. He'd purposefully waited to walk back with her, though she very much doubted chivalry—or attraction—had anything to do with the man's motives. She was definitely not his type.

"So why would someone like you want to do ghoul work?"

He shifted the plastic grocery bag stuffed with sandwiches and drinks he'd taken from a cooler on the porch to the other hand. "Don't you ever get creeped out by what you do?"

"You're in law enforcement," Erin said. "Don't tell me you get all squeamish at the sight of a few bones."

"Hell, no. But the way you've been digging around in the dirt all morning—I wouldn't exactly call that woman's work, would you?"

Arrogant *and* chauvinistic. Lovely. Erin's favorite combination. She shoved a limb out of her way with more vehemence than necessary.

"So who do you think those bones belong to?" Avery was trying to sound casual, but there was an undercurrent of something in his voice that sent a prickle of alarm down Erin's backbone. Was this why he'd waited for her—to interrogate her?

"I won't know that until I have a chance to examine them more thoroughly," she said.

"I bet you have some idea. Come on. Gallagher said something to you, didn't he? Gave you a hint. How'd he get you to come all the way out here?"

"I came because this is my job," Erin told him briskly. "I've consulted on dozens of cases like this."

"Cases like what?"

Again that underlying tone that had an edge of intrigue to it. He seemed to be fishing, but Erin couldn't imagine why. Was his interest in the remains something other than professional?

The notion made her more than a little uneasy, and she had to resist the urge to keep glancing over her shoulder. She wished they could trade places, because all of a sudden, she had no desire to have Clive Avery at her back.

"You must have some idea yourself," she said, turning the tables on him. "You can't have had that many disappearances in this area."

"Lot of people from the city come out here to hunt and fish. Some come out here to take care of business, if you know what I mean. We can't keep track of all their comings and goings." The underbrush crunched beneath his boots. "Besides, these woods are big and thick. They go on for miles. Pretty good place to dump a body."

"You think the deceased was murdered someplace else and then dumped here?"

"Don't you?" Avery asked.

Erin knew she shouldn't discuss the possibility. "We won't know that until the remains have been thoroughly examined," she said quickly.

She had a pretty good idea, however. The moment she'd excavated the skull, the evidence had been glaring. She couldn't believe the others hadn't noticed, but then, except for Jamie who was taking pictures, they'd all tried to avoid looking at the bones.

Jamie had commented on the missing teeth, but Erin wasn't sure he understood the significance of what he'd seen and photographed, nor did she think the others had heard him. They were all too busy concentrating on their own tasks.

Trying to cover her momentary lapse, she said, "So have you always lived around here?"

He gave a disgusted grunt as he snapped a twig in two. "No way. I'm a big-city man myself."

"Chicago?"

His hesitation was infinitesimal, but Erin sensed she'd hit a nerve. "What is this, an inquisition?"

She shrugged. "Just curious."

"Curious, huh?" She heard the amusement in his tone, and realized he'd interpreted her curiosity as interest. He would. "So you married?" he asked in a none too subtle tone.

"No."

"Involved?"

Erin frowned. "I don't think we need to get personal, do we?"

He gave a low chuckle. "Which means you aren't. Attached women can't wait to crow about it."

Erin rolled her eyes again. The man's condescension was beyond irritating.

"What about you and supercop?" he persisted.

"You mean Detective Gallagher? What about us?" Erin said coolly.

"The two of you got something going or what?"

Her pulse raced, all of a sudden. "Not that it's any of your business, but we only met yesterday."

''That so?'' He grabbed her arm, turning her around to face him.

Erin jerked her arm from his grasp. ''What do you think you're doing?''

''Just thought we could stop here and talk for a little while. You know, get to know each other better.''

''We've been talking.''

He grinned down at her. ''Okay, no talking then.''

He bent his head toward hers, as if to kiss her, and Erin stepped quickly away from him. He laughed, but there was a flash of surprise in his eyes, as if he wasn't accustomed to being turned down—certainly not by the likes of her. Surprise but not anger, Erin noted, because his pass had been purely instinctual, motivated more by habit than by attraction.

Or was he putting the moves on her for another reason? What did he hope to gain if he seduced her? An inside track on her investigation?

''Ah, come on, doc. Lighten up. Don't tell me you're one of those frigid, egghead types.''

Without a word, Erin turned and started down the path, shoving another limb out of her path. But instead of handing the branch off to Avery, as she'd done earlier, she let it snap back like a catapult. The limb slapped the deputy across the face with a loud *whack,* and he let out a string of expletives the like of which Erin had not heard since her years in a dorm.

She glanced back contritely. ''Sorry. The darn thing slipped right out of my hand.''

THEY'D EATEN a hasty lunch, the bones had been packed for travel, and the last of the dirt sifted by the time the rain started that afternoon. It came slowly, in fat, icy drops that splattered against Erin's face as she glanced skyward. "Looks like we finished just in time."

For the past couple of hours, Nick had been silent, working the sifter with a fierce concentration that was hardly warranted for such a mundane task. Surprisingly, it was Jamie who offered his assistance when Erin had begun to pack up the bones. He and the sheriff then headed back to the cabin with the remains while Erin gathered up her equipment.

Clive Avery, an angry red welt marring his sullen expression, followed soon after, leaving Erin and Nick alone in the clearing. She saw that he was staring at the indention in the ground where the skeleton had been removed.

Something in his face, a raw vulnerability that seemed out of character for him, made Erin's heart give a funny skip, and when his gaze met hers, everything tilted inside her, as if something in her narrow, little world had been irrevocably changed.

"Thank you," he said into the waiting stillness.

She made a tiny gesture with her hand. "You don't need to thank me. This is what I do."

"It's the way you do it."

She understood what he meant. "The absence of skin, tissue, or muscle doesn't lessen the humanity for me. I care about them all."

For a split second, she thought he wanted to say something else to her, but he shrugged instead and turned away from her. But before he could hide it, Erin had glimpsed an emotion in his blue eyes that almost looked like grief.

She wondered, not for the first time, what she would find—*who* she would find—once she began her examination of the bones.

Chapter Five

They could see the rain ahead of them, like a heavy, gray veil trailing down from the heavens. Nick took both the canvas bags of equipment, and motioned Erin to move in front of him in the woods. "We'd better hurry."

But by the time they reached the cabin, they were both drenched and the ground oozed with mud. They ran up the wooden steps, shivering in their wet clothes as they deposited their gear on the porch.

"Looks like what you-all down south call a real gully washer," Roy Glass remarked mildly to Erin. He pulled out a pack of cigarettes, shook one out, and then lit up, tossing the match into the rain.

"Maybe we should go ahead and make a run for the cars," she suggested. "This doesn't look like it's going to let up any time soon."

"We won't be going anywhere for a while." He blew a lazy stream of smoke from the side of his mouth. "Clive just talked to dispatch. We've got flash flooding over the highway between here and town, and the dirt road we came in on is likely knee-deep in mud."

"You mean we're stranded out here?" Erin asked

incredulously. Now that the excavation was completed, she was anxious to get back to the lab and begin the next phase.

And, if she was truthful with herself, the woods were starting to get to her. She couldn't seem to shake the feeling of dread that had dogged her since she'd begun the excavation, and even more so since she'd seen the condition of the skeleton.

"It happens," Roy said with a shrug. "What should we do with the bones in the meantime, doc?"

"Let's put them inside," she said. "Make sure they stay dry and as undisturbed as possible."

"We can use one of the bedrooms." Nick's voice sounded tense, as if he were working very hard to control his emotions. Erin glanced up at him, but he avoided her gaze.

Several minutes later, the two deputies scurried out of the woods from the direction of the road, their heads lowered against the rain. Water dripped off the brims of their hats as they ran up the steps, taking refuge on the porch with the rest of them.

"Road's out," Avery said, taking off his wet jacket and shaking it out.

Jamie, his teeth chattering from the cold, nodded in agreement. "He's right, Sheriff. It looks pretty bad."

"What about the cars?"

"We moved the cruisers up the road to higher ground," Avery said. "Maybe you two better do the same."

Nick nodded. "The rest of you may as well go inside, see if you can get a fire going so we can all dry out." To Erin, he said, "I'll be back in a few minutes."

She wiped a wet strand of hair from her face, and

then, without knowing why, she caught his arm. "Be careful out there."

If he thought her warning odd, he didn't say so. He gazed at her for a moment before turning to run down the steps. Erin was left alone with the sheriff and his two deputies, none of whom she'd ever laid eyes on before that morning, but one of whom she'd managed to make a deadly enemy.

Clive Avery was staring at her, smiling.

NICK BROUGHT their bags from the car, and the two of them were at least able to change into dry clothing. Roy, Avery, and Jamie all sat huddled before the fireplace, trying to dry out as best they could.

Darkness came early because of the storm, and as evening wore on, they ate the remainder of the sandwiches from the cooler and drank coffee prepared from the cabin's meager reserves.

The rain refused to let up, and the five of them settled in for the night. Avery used his cell phone to call the station again, confirming that dozens of people all over the county were stranded by the flash flooding. The absence of the sheriff and two deputies severely depleted the area's police force, but there was nothing to be done about that.

Around ten o'clock, having played cards until they were sick of each other's company, the two deputies stretched out on cots in the main area of the cabin, and the sheriff took the couch. Nick had stored Erin's bag in the second bedroom earlier, and she turned to him now, watching him put away the deck of cards where he'd found it.

"Where will you sleep?" she asked him.

He shrugged, but his gaze looked uneasy. "I don't plan to sleep much."

"Look, there's no point in your having to stay awake all night," Erin said. "There're two beds in my room. We're both adults." Then realizing how that sounded, she said quickly, "I mean, there's no good reason why we can't share the same room."

For the first time all day, she thought she saw amusement in his gaze. "Do you sleep with your hair down?"

"Wh-what?"

He seemed to reconsider the question, and his hand—which Erin could have sworn was reaching for her hair—dropped to his side. "Never mind. Why don't you go ahead and get some rest? If I get tired, I'll stretch out by the fireplace. Don't worry about me."

But Erin's sleep was far from restful. She never dreamed about her work, but there was a nightmarish quality to her visions that night that had her sleeping fitfully and waking sporadically. Once, she saw a face staring through the window at her. At first she thought it was Ralph, the security guard at the lab, but then his features changed and she saw Clive Avery laughing through the glass at her. Then the face altered again, and it was Ed Dawson outside her window, his gaze cold and deadly.

For an eternity, Erin stared mesmerized at the morphing visage in her window. She couldn't tell if she was asleep or awake, and when she tried to move, she found that her arms and legs were tightly bound. She tried to sit up, but the walls and ceiling of the room closed in on her until she was lying in some sort of box.

Not a box, she realized in horror, but a coffin.

Gasping for breath, Erin bolted upright in bed and gazed around the darkened room. What had awakened her? The nightmare? A sound?

She listened to the darkness, her heart still pounding. The rain had let up sometime during the night. In the silence that followed, she could hear a tree limb raking the side of the cabin in the wind, and a fainter sound that might have been footsteps sloshing in mud.

Erin caught her breath. Was someone walking around outside the cabin? Someone wanting shelter from the storm perhaps, or someone with far more sinister intent?

Even as the notion crossed her mind, another noise came to her, a furtive, scraping sound of metal against wood, as if someone were trying to pry open a window.

Blood pounding, Erin swung her legs off the bed, hesitating a moment before pulling on her jeans. It was crazy to be so alarmed, she told herself. There were no less than four armed lawmen outside her bedroom door. She was as safe as the gold in Fort Knox, but...it wasn't really her security she was worried about, she realized suddenly. What if someone had known the conclusions she would reach when she examined the skeleton? What if someone had decided to destroy the evidence before she could report her findings? Before she could testify in a court of law?

Crossing the room to the window, Erin glanced out. Though the rain had slacked, the night was still dark and stormy, the heavy cloud coverage blocking the moon. A ground mist hovered at the edge of the woods, and Erin could see only nebulous shadows in the gloom. But as her eyes became accustomed to the dark, she saw a motion near the trees that caused the mist to swirl. A limb blowing in the wind? An animal caught out in the storm?

A man, darkly dressed, moving quickly away from the cabin.

As Erin watched, the figure disappeared into the trees, but she had the uncanny feeling that he hadn't gone far. He was out there, she thought, waiting for an opportunity to get inside.

Turning away from the window, Erin finished dressing, then slipped out her bedroom door. The glow of coals in the fireplace did little to illuminate the room, and she paused, glancing around to get her bearings. She could hear the deep, even breathing from the direction of the cots, Roy Glass's soft snoring from the sofa, but the sounds were far from comforting. Had she been the only one to sense danger?

Erin wondered if she should rouse them, but she remembered the ridicule Jamie had gotten for his panic the night before. She didn't really care what Clive Avery thought of her, but she didn't relish drawing Nick's scorn, particularly after the incident with Ralph in the lab earlier. Still, if an intruder was skulking about outside, she needed to alert someone.

The front door opened suddenly, and Erin gasped, her hand flying to her heart. In the split second before she recognized Nick standing in the doorway, she jumped back, stumbling over a wooden chair that went crashing backward to the floor. The noise, if not loud enough to wake the dead, was certainly sufficient to rouse the sleeping lawmen. Erin could hear them scrambling out of their makeshift beds, no doubt instinctively reaching for their weapons.

"Sorry," she muttered.

"What the hell's going on?" Roy thundered, and she

heard Clive Avery swear. Judging from their tones, Erin was lucky she hadn't already been shot.

Nick came inside, closing the door behind him, but he didn't turn on the light. He walked across the room toward Erin. "You all right?"

She nodded, then realizing he couldn't see her in the dark, she said, "I thought I heard something, so I came out to investigate. When you opened the door, it...startled me. I stumbled against a chair."

"Heard what?" Avery demanded. Erin could barely make out his silhouette, but she had the impression that he was fully alert. There was none of the drowsiness in his voice that she'd heard in Roy Glass's. Had Avery only been pretending to sleep? Had he heard the noise, too?

"I thought someone was trying to break into the cabin," she said.

Avery stalked across the floor and flipped the light switch, but nothing happened. "What the hell—?"

"Storm must have knocked out the electricity," Roy said glumly. "What's this about someone trying to break into the cabin?"

"She may be right," Nick said. "Someone was outside."

So the figure she'd seen moving toward the woods hadn't been her imagination. What about the face in her bedroom window?

"How do you know someone was outside?" Avery challenged Nick.

"I heard something, too," he said. "When I went outside to have a look, I saw footprints in the mud, around by the bedroom windows. They had to have been made since the rain let up." Nick glanced around the room suddenly. "Where's Jamie?"

His question startled them all, and as if one, their gazes roamed the room, then came back to settle uneasily on each other.

"Did you hear him go out?" Roy Glass asked Avery.

"I didn't see or hear anything," he said almost angrily. "We've got a bunch of wild imaginations around here if you ask me. Jamie's probably in the john."

But when he walked over and banged on the bathroom door, there was no response. He shrugged. "Maybe he went out to get some air."

Erin, shivering in the chilly gloom, wrapped her arms around her middle. "Maybe he heard the noise, too, and went out to investigate. When I looked out the bedroom window, I saw someone walking toward the woods."

"There you go," Avery said. "You probably saw Jamie going for a walk. Those were probably his footprints in the mud."

"I don't think so," Nick said slowly. "The prints I saw were deep, made by a much larger man."

"Then maybe it was a bum, trying to get in out of the rain," Avery insisted. Why he was so resistant to the notion of an intruder, Erin couldn't imagine.

"Maybe," Nick said. "But why didn't he try the front door if he thought the cabin was deserted? Why try to break in through a window? The back bedroom window to be exact," he added ominously.

"Are you saying you think he was after the skeleton?" Avery asked incredulously. "That's crazy."

"Is it?" Nick's tone was cold, and though she couldn't see him clearly, Erin could imagine his icy glare, directed at Avery. "If the victim was murdered, the remains are evidence."

"That's crazy," Avery said again, and this time, Erin thought she detected an edge that might have been desperation. "Those bones were probably buried out there for years. Who'd even remember?"

"The killer," Nick said quietly.

"You're assuming a helluva lot, aren't you?" Avery demanded.

"Maybe we can't afford not to assume," Nick said. "If the killer somehow found out the remains had been recovered, doesn't it stand to reason he'd do everything in his power to obstruct Dr. Casey's investigation?"

The chill inside Erin deepened, and the dread she'd been experiencing for hours descended over her again. She sensed their eyes on her in the darkness, making her feel as if she needed to say or do something to assure them she was up to the challenge.

She moistened her lips. "Nick's right," she finally said. "I have reason to believe the man inside that room met with foul play. If someone tampers with the remains, crucial evidence could be destroyed. We can't let that happen."

The room seemed to hold a collective breath for a tense moment, then Roy Glass said in a hushed, reverent voice, "You said 'the man inside that room.' You know that for a fact, doc?"

"I'm ninety-nine percent certain the remains are male," Erin said.

Her eyes were becoming accustomed to the gloom, and she could almost make out their faces now. She thought she saw Nick and Roy Glass exchange glances.

"You know he was murdered?" This, sharply, from Clive Avery. "You saw a bullet wound? A bashed in skull? What?"

"Nothing that obvious, I'm afraid. I still don't know

the cause or manner of death." Although she had noted some damage to the skull.

"Then how do you know he met with foul play?"

Erin hesitated, uncertain how much she should tell them. But they'd all been present at the excavation. They'd all had the opportunity to observe what she'd seen. She glanced at Nick. "The teeth are all missing, which isn't necessarily unusual for remains that have been exposed to the elements for a long period of time, more than five years I'd say in this case. But we didn't find any of the teeth when we sifted through the dirt, and in addition, the mandible—the lower jawbone—is so badly damaged that a positive identification using dental records is virtually impossible."

"That's why you said you think the victim met with foul play," Roy Glass said quietly. "Someone went to the trouble to make sure he couldn't be identified."

"It seems suspect," Erin agreed. "Although the damage could have been done by animals. I won't know that for certain until I can use a microscope and X rays."

"In the meantime, you and Nick both thought you heard someone trying to break into the cabin," Roy mused. "I don't believe we can regard that as a coincidence."

"I still say you're all making a mountain out of a mole hill," Avery grumbled. "In case you've all forgotten, we're stranded out here. How the hell could an intruder get through the water when we can't?"

"By boat, maybe," Roy said grimly.

"Or maybe he was already here before the water started rising," Nick said.

They all fell silent again, digesting the possibilities. The idea of someone being out here, watching them…

Erin shivered, watching Nick in the darkness. She could feel his eyes on her, too, and her stomach fluttered, both in fear and awareness.

"I'd feel a lot better if we knew where Jamie was," Roy said. "He's still pretty green. After the razzing he took earlier, if he did hear something, he might have gone out to investigate by himself to make sure it wasn't a deer or something before he awakened the rest of us."

"Then we'd better go out and take a look around for him," Nick said.

Erin expected Avery to protest, but to her surprise, she saw him reach for his jacket. "Wait'll I get my hands on that little..." he trailed off, but they all got the gist of his threat.

Nick turned to Erin. "Stay inside," he said, "and lock the door behind us."

Although Erin didn't much relish being left behind, she was also the only one unarmed and untrained for such risks. If there was an intruder out there somewhere, it didn't make much sense for her to go traipsing about the woods. She nodded and moved toward the door.

One by one, the three of them filed out into the darkness. Avery was the last. When he passed by Erin, his jacket brushed her arm. The cloth was damp, almost wet, although she distinctly remembered him hanging it by the fireplace earlier to dry.

Had he been out in the rain while the rest of them slept? Had he been the one gazing in her bedroom window?

ERIN TRIED to fight off her uneasiness as she glanced around the deserted cabin. Crossing the room, she stirred the embers in the fireplace, then tossed another log on the glowing coals. The fire caught almost instantly and snapped to life, forcing the shadows on the walls and ceiling into a macabre dance.

Erin warmed herself by the blaze for a moment as she stared at the closed bedroom door, behind which rested the remains of a man she might or might not be able to identify. She hadn't told the others everything she'd discovered that day simply because she couldn't explain her findings. Apart from the missing teeth and the damaged mandible, she couldn't yet tell them why she was certain the man had been murdered, only that she was. And her instincts for such things were rarely wrong.

She walked over and opened the bedroom door, staring into the darkened interior. After a moment, light from the fireplace penetrated the gloom, and Erin could make out the silhouette of furniture, the glint of glass at the window. The bones were still packed carefully away and hadn't been touched since the two deputies had carried them inside earlier that day. If someone had been trying to get to them, how had he or she known they would be in this cabin, in this very room?

A memory glimmered then took hold. Clive Avery had been talking on his cell phone when Erin had come out of the woods. He'd closed the phone quickly as if he hadn't wanted her to overhear any of his conversation. Had he summoned someone to the cabin before the rain started?

She stood staring down at the bones, that nameless dread forming inside her again. ''Who are you?'' she whispered into the darkness.

Whoever he was, it was becoming apparent to Erin that he was as much a threat in death as he had been in life. And it was up to her to unlock his secrets before his murderer could cover his tracks yet again.

NICK FOLLOWED the footsteps in the mud away from the cabin, but near the edge of the woods, the trail was quickly swallowed by the mist. He glanced back at the cabin. It looked dark and deserted, and for a moment, he had to fight the urge to go back and make sure Erin was okay. But she was inside, the door was locked, and he, Roy and Avery were patrolling the area, looking for Jamie. No one could get back to the cabin without being spotted. Unless, of course, the intruder had never left…

Don't get paranoid, a grim voice told him. But he couldn't shake the feeling of unease this place always caused him. Bad enough his father had disappeared from the cabin, but then, a few months ago, his brother, Tony, had been lured out here by a madman who had kidnapped their sister, Fiona, and Tony's partner, Eve Barrett. Both women had been held hostage by their would-be killer while he set a trap for Tony. But instead of coming through the door, or even one of the lower windows, as expected, Tony had climbed to the roof and lain in wait himself, watching his quarry through the old-fashioned skylight until the precise moment he could strike.

Nick's pulse quickened as he tried to scan the roofline in the darkness. Erin was in danger. The thought came to him instantly, and he didn't take time to analyze where it had come from or why he was so certain. He'd learned a long time ago to follow his instincts.

Abandoning the woods, he headed quickly back toward the cabin. Somewhere to the left of him, he could hear the sheriff calling to Jamie, but his voice was so muted by the mist, he seemed a long way off.

Nick had no idea where Clive Avery was, but he had a suspicion the man had not followed them into the woods. Instead, the deputy had doubled back to the cabin. To Erin. Nick had seen the way he'd looked at her earlier, seen Erin's expression when the two of them had come out of the woods. Something had happened between them, and by the welt on Avery's face, Erin had more than held her own. But Avery didn't strike Nick as the type of man who would be bested by a woman and let it pass—

In his haste, he tripped over a log and went sprawling into the mud. His flashlight hit the ground and went out. Swearing, Nick pushed himself off the wet ground, placing his hand on the log for balance. The wood was warm and pliable. Not a log at all, but a body.

The adrenaline poured through Nick's veins as he shook his flashlight almost viciously until the bulb came on again. The light flickered weakly, then caught, gleaming against a metal badge on a brown jacket.

He thought at first it was Jamie, but then as Nick moved in closer, the light struck blond hair and staring green eyes.

Avery...

Chapter Six

"Dead?" Erin stared at Nick in shock. *"Clive Avery is dead? My God! How? When?"* The questions tumbled out of her, subduing the terror she'd experienced when Nick had started pounding on the cabin door only moments before. She hadn't let him in until he'd called out her name and she'd recognized his voice.

The light from the fireplace flickered over him, and Erin could see that his clothes were streaked with dirt and blood, and the terror came back full force. She gasped in shock. "Dead," she repeated almost in a whisper. "How?"

He hesitated, then said, "His throat was cut."

Erin's hand flew to her mouth. "Oh my *God.* Then someone really did try to break into the cabin. Nick, what are we going to do?"

"We're going to keep him out." Nick moved passed her to the window, staring out. He didn't put away his weapon, but kept it ready at his side.

Erin didn't want to show her fear, but she was terrified. She wasn't used to danger. Her work kept her in the lab mostly. The victims she saw there had usually been dead for a long time. But Clive Avery lay just outside the cabin, his throat viciously slashed.

She steeled her nerves. "Are you certain he's dead? Should we try to get him to a doctor?"

"He doesn't need a doctor, Erin, trust me." Nick glanced at her over his shoulder. "Besides, the roads are impassable, remember? We couldn't get a doctor or medical examiner out here for hours, maybe days, let alone a CSU team. All we can do is secure the area as best we can, but with all this rain—" He saw her face and hesitated. "Are you okay? Did you hear anything while I was gone? See anything?"

"No, nothing." Erin tried to suppress a shudder. "Where's Roy? And Jamie?"

"Still out there somewhere. I'm going back out to find them. But I had to make sure you were safe first. I thought—" He broke off again and glanced out the window.

But somehow Erin knew what he was thinking. He'd believed she was in danger and he'd come back for her.

Her heart skipped a beat as she gazed up at him. She caught his arm almost desperately. "I know you're not telling me everything. Who killed Avery?"

He gave her a grim look. "I wish I knew. Lock the door behind me. And don't open it under any circumstances unless you hear my voice. Only *my* voice. Do you understand?"

His meaning hit her like a physical blow. *Don't open the door unless you hear my voice. Only my voice.* Which meant that she was not to trust Roy or Jamie. But surely Nick didn't suspect either of them of Avery's murder? They were all colleagues—

Slowly, she nodded. "I understand." When he would have turned away, she said, "Be careful, Nick, please."

He didn't say anything, but in the dancing light, she could see the grim determination in his eyes, the cold resolution of his features. Erin shivered as she watched him open the door and disappear once again into the wet darkness.

Alone again, she glanced around the empty cabin, unsure what to do, how to keep her mind busy and free of panic. She walked over to the fireplace and warmed herself as she tried to set her mind to work on the current problem. Who had killed Avery?

Erin had assumed the noise she'd heard outside and the figure she'd seen hurrying toward the woods had been an intruder. But what if the person she'd seen had been one of them? Avery's jacket had been wet earlier, as if he'd been outside sometime during the night. But now Avery was dead. Jamie was still missing. Roy Glass was out there somewhere, and so was Nick. If Roy or Jamie was the murderer, Nick could be in real trouble.

Erin fought back another wave of panic as she concentrated even harder on the problem. It made no sense for Roy or Jamie to have killed Avery. They weren't connected to the skeleton. Assuming, of course, Avery's murder had been motivated by the discovery of the remains. It was possible his death could be completely unrelated. Erin had no doubt Clive Avery had made enemies along the way. Men like him usually did. Perhaps the attempted break-in had been a ruse, a way to lure him outside.

The flooding had isolated the cabin. So whoever was out there had either been there all day, watching them, or he knew another way in and out of the woods. A local man? A professional? The possibilities were more dire than Erin cared to dwell on.

Another thought came to her. What if Erin herself was the target? Hadn't Lois Childers warned her last night that her appointment as head of FAHIL had been met with hostility from Russell Quay?

But try as she might, Erin couldn't bring herself to believe the diminutive little man could be a murderer. He seemed so harmless.

That's the kind you have to watch out for.

As Lois's warning raced through Erin's mind, the soft knocking at the door seemed at first to be a part of her imagination, a sound conjured by her fear. But the knocking came again, and Erin's heart caught in her throat as she moved from her spot near the fire to place her ear against the door. The knock was soft, furtive, almost desperate. Like an echo of her heartbeat.

"Dr. Casey...Erin? Open the door. Hurry!" The voice was muted, as if the speaker was deliberately trying to disguise his identity, but not enough so as to alarm her. She could neither place nor discount the voice as Roy's or Jamie's—or even Russell Quay's, for that matter—although there was an edge of familiarity to the tone that seemed to touch a memory, long buried, inside her.

"It's Sheriff Glass," the voice said urgently. "Open up."

Sheriff Glass. Not Roy, as he'd told her to call him earlier.

Erin's blood pounded in her ears as she listened to the silence that followed the knock. Slowly, she dropped her gaze and saw the doorknob turn.

She put her hand on the metal, not certain what she would do if the killer tried to force his way in. But the lock held, and after a moment, the soft thud of footsteps sounded across the wooden porch.

But Erin knew he hadn't gone far. If Clive Avery's murderer had come back for the remains of another of his victims, then Erin was the only one who now stood in his way.

She whirled, rushing toward the back bedroom to check the window. The lock was still in place, but Erin knew that wouldn't stop someone desperate to get inside. Leaving the room almost reluctantly, she checked the window in her bedroom, then the one in the living area, and for good measure, the door again. The cabin was as secure as she could make it, and for a moment, she let herself believe that she would be safe until Nick came back.

Then she heard the sound on the roof, a *thunk* that could either have been a pinecone falling from a tree…or a misplaced footstep in the darkness.

THE BODY WAS MISSING, and Roy and Jamie were nowhere to be found. It was as if the three lawmen—two presumably still alive—had disappeared off the face of the earth.

Nick had been in dicey situations before. He knew how to deal with nerves. He used the adrenaline kick in his veins to sharpen his senses, to keep himself edgy and ready as he eased through the darkness.

Someone had murdered Clive Avery and then removed the body. For all Nick knew, the killer could have gotten to Roy and Jamie, as well. Maybe the murderer was lying in wait, picking them off one by one, willing to kill over and over in order to cover the tracks another killer left eight years ago.

You son of a bitch. I'm coming for you.

Nick didn't use his flashlight, but moved as steadily as he could at the edge of the woods, using the low-lying fog as cover. The mist was both his curse and his salvation. He couldn't track the killer's footprints in the mud, but neither could the killer shadow him. Nick kept on the move, pausing every few minutes to listen to the darkness, but all was silent except for the steady drip from the trees, the hoot of an owl in the distance.

He'd inadvertently widened his circle, and now as Nick glanced back toward the cabin, he realized he'd gone farther than he meant to. The structure was only a vague shadow against the darker blackness of the woods. There was a window in front, but from this distance, he couldn't see anything inside. But he could imagine Erin standing by the fire, worried, frightened, but not panicky. She could handle herself. In spite of her size, she was one of the most competent women Nick had ever known.

Even so, he found himself hurrying his steps, anxious to get back to the cabin. To Erin. She was in danger. They were all in danger, and for a moment, Nick let himself speculate on the possibility that the murderer could be someone other than who he suspected. What if Avery's death had nothing to do with the discovery of the remains?

But he didn't believe that to be the case. He knew who was out in these woods, or at least, who had put the killer onto their trail. Richard O'Roarke was desperate to get his only son out of prison. He would do anything to make sure Daniel wasn't implicated in another murder. What was another dead body or two to the O'Roarkes?

And even though Daniel was on death row, he still had access to the outside world through visitors, e-mail and the telephone. Maybe this was his doing. Maybe he'd somehow found out Sean Gallagher's remains had been discovered, and had ordered one of his minions to do his dirty work. O'Roarke was a celebrity now. He commanded even more power. Even in prison, murder was not beyond his reach.

A few minutes later, Nick found Roy Glass about thirty feet out from the cabin. He'd been bashed in the head, and judging by the cuts on his arms and face, he'd put up one helluva a fight. He was still alive, but barely. His breathing was shallow, his heartbeat irregular. The killer must have been scared off, either by Nick or Jamie, before he'd had a chance to finish the job.

Nick had two choices. Wait to see if the killer came back and get the jump on him, or carry Roy back to the safety of the cabin, which meant Nick would have to put away his weapon. For whatever time it took him to haul ass with Roy across the clearing, the two of them would be exposed to the killer.

He gazed down into Roy's bloodstained face. There really wasn't a choice after all.

ERIN'S GAZE went to the skylight. There was no moon or stars, so all she could see was blackness. The light from the fireplace reflected against the glass, creating an illusion of movement that almost stopped her heart.

She didn't dare move a muscle, but stood completely still, listening for the telltale sound of another footstep. Blood drummed in her ears, but she tried to keep herself calm, tried to figure out exactly what she would do if someone came crashing through the skylight.

Run! a voice inside her screamed.

She cut her gaze to the door. If the killer was on the roof, Erin could go outside, sprint for the woods, scream for Nick and Roy and Jamie. They would all come running toward the cabin. The killer would be trapped on the roof.

Or...

He was still standing outside the door. The sound on the roof had been a diversion, a stone tossed onto the shingles to make her think he was up there. Then when she opened the door...

Erin could feel the panic welling inside her as she gazed at the skylight, then the door. The skylight, then the door. *Where are you?* she wanted to scream. The silence inside the cabin was almost deafening.

The banging sounded again at the front door, and Erin started violently. She backed away, putting herself directly under the skylight. And then, a fraction of a second before she heard Nick's voice, she saw a shadow move across the glass. The killer was up there!

And Nick was at the front door. Erin flew across the room to let him in, but then paused, her hand hovering over the lock.

"Erin! Open up!"

The voice sounded muted, strained. Not entirely like Nick's.

"Erin! Open the door!" An edge of impatience that was unmistakable.

She said softly through the wood, "How do I know it's you?"

An exasperated silence. Then, "Indiana Jones," he said almost angrily. "I know all about Indiana Jones."

She twisted the lock and opened the door. Nick stumbled inside with Roy Glass draped over his shoulder. The man's weight was undoubtedly what had caused the strain in Nick's voice.

"Oh my God," she breathed. "Is he—"

"He's still alive."

Quickly, Erin closed and locked the door behind Nick. Before he could say anything else, she put her hand on his arm and pointed to the skylight. "He's up there."

Nick nodded and placed the sheriff none too gently on the couch before the fire. Without a word, he drew his weapon, gazing up at the skylight. When Erin would have spoken, he silenced her with a finger to his lips.

Her heart still thundering, Erin moved to the unconscious sheriff, examining the wound on the side of his head as best she could in the firelight. She felt his pulse, reassuring herself he was still alive.

Nick said against her ear, "I'm going up to have a look."

Before Erin could ask him what he meant, he headed across the room, opening the door to the bedroom in which she'd slept earlier. He disappeared inside, and after a moment, Erin heard the window ease open. She left her place by Roy and went to the doorway.

Standing on the sill, Nick hoisted himself up to the roof. For a split second, his legs dangled in front of the window, and then he was gone. Erin listened for his footsteps on the roof, but he was as silent as the killer.

She shivered, waiting, half expecting to hear a gunshot or some sign of a struggle. But after less than two minutes, Nick swung himself back through the window.

"If he was up there, he's gone now," he said, slamming home the window and locking it. He turned back to Erin. "We're in trouble here, Erin."

She nodded. "I know." Then without another word, she turned and walked back over to check on Roy. He was still unconscious, his heartbeat still very weak. "What happened to him?"

"Looks like he was jumped from behind, but he was able to put up a struggle. Probably saved his life." Nick brought a towel from the bathroom and placed it on the wound on Roy's skull, although the bleeding had almost stopped. Together, they cleaned the cuts on his face and arms as best they could. Defense wounds, Erin thought. Luckily, most of them were superficial.

"What about Jamie?"

Nick shook his head. "I didn't see any sign of him. I'm hoping he got scared and bolted. He's probably lived around here all his life. He knows these woods."

But he didn't sound very convincing, and Erin knew that he was thinking the same thing she was. Jamie was the first one to disappear. He'd heard the noise, gone out to investigate, and been ambushed. He was lying out there dead, just like Clive Avery, and just like Roy Glass would have been, if not for the grace of God.

And now she and Nick were still trapped in the cabin. Even if they could make it to the cars, the roads were flooded. There was nowhere to go.

She glanced up at Nick. "Clive Avery had a cell phone," she said. "I saw him put it in his jacket pocket earlier. Maybe we could use it to call for help."

"I've already tried mine. The signal's too weak, and I can't charge the battery without electricity."

"But maybe Clive's—"

"His body has disappeared from where I saw it earlier. Presumably his phone along with it."

Erin felt a shiver go through her. The murderer was already covering his tracks. Not only vicious, but cold and calculating. Perhaps there was even more than one.

Erin glanced at Nick. "The radios in the squad cars?"

"I thought of that," he said. "But if we leave the cabin, we're completely exposed. And there's no guarantee the radios haven't been destroyed."

"So we're trapped," she said almost numbly.

"Trapped but not helpless." He drew Roy Glass's weapon from his holster, checked the clip, then handed the gun to Erin.

She took it without hesitation. When he started to instruct her on how to handle it, she said, "I know how to use it. My mother and I both took classes." Because they were two women living alone, Madeline had told her, but Erin had always suspected it was because her mother remained afraid of Erin's father. Afraid he would someday come for Erin.

She needn't have worried, Erin thought with a trace of bitterness. Her father had forgotten she existed.

"We sit tight until morning," Nick said as he stirred the fire. He threw on another log, causing sparks to pop like tiny firecrackers. "Maybe by then the water will be receding and we can get out of here."

But no sooner had he said the words, than Erin glanced up at the sputtering sound against the skylight. "Listen," she said. "It's raining again."

They stared at each other in the gloom.

THE MINUTES CREPT BY. Erin kept herself busy at first by tending to Roy, finding a blanket to cover him, taking his pulse. But after awhile, there was nothing more she could do for him, so she sat by the fire and watched Nick pace. He was a restless man, and she wondered how he ever managed surveillance work.

She said into the silence, "Whose cabin is this, Nick?"

Her voice seemed to startle him. He didn't answer her for a long moment, then, almost reluctantly, he came to sit by her at the fire. "I told you. It belongs to some people I know."

"It looks as if the windows were recently boarded up. Do they ever come here?"

"Not very often."

He seemed hesitant to talk about the owners, and Erin couldn't help wondering why. "Do they know we're here?"

He shook his head. "No. No one in the department knows where I am, either. Roy and I agreed to keep the discovery of the remains and the excavation as quiet as possible."

"Why?"

"We had our reasons."

Erin drew up her legs, wrapping her arms around them as she rested her chin on her knees. "Obviously, you didn't keep it quiet enough. Someone found out, unless this is all some strange, horrible coincidence. That's possible, isn't it?" She lifted her head and glanced at him hopefully.

"What do you mean?"

"Whoever killed Clive Avery and attacked Roy. It might not have anything to do with the remains. It could be some psycho out there roaming the woods."

Nick looked faintly amused. "That would make you feel better?"

She saw his point. "No, I guess not. I even thought for a while—"

When she broke off, he glanced at her sharply. "What?"

She gave him a weak smile. "It crossed my mind that someone might be after me. Not everyone at Hillsboro is thrilled to have me on board."

"There's been trouble?"

She hesitated. "No. Just a warning or two. But I can't imagine anyone being upset enough by my appointment to murder an innocent man just to get to me."

"I doubt Avery was all that innocent," Nick said dryly.

"What makes you say that?"

His shrug was the only answer she got.

Erin sat facing the fire, but Nick had his back to the hearth, so that he could see the entire room. When he turned toward her, firelight danced over his features, emphasizing the bone structure in his face—the high cheekbones, the strong jawline, the stubborn chin. His gun rested on the floor beside him. Roy Glass's weapon was on the hearth. They were ready, Erin tried to tell herself, but in truth, she wasn't sure how quickly she would react if the cabin came under attack.

"Do you think Jamie is still alive?" she asked him.

"I don't know. It's possible he did his job, then hightailed it out of here. Someone inside the sheriff's department talked, Erin. No one else knew about the remains or the excavation. Except for you and me, of course. Maybe it was Jamie."

Erin thought about that. "When I came back to the cabin this afternoon, I saw Avery talking on his cell phone. I got the distinct impression he didn't want me overhearing his conversation. I would have guessed him to be the leak, but now that he's dead, that clears him, doesn't it?"

"Not necessarily. Maybe he served his purpose, and

he was one more piece of evidence that had to be gotten rid of.''

''Which brings us back to the remains. Who is he, Nick? Who is in that room?''

His gaze looked even more intense in the firelight. ''That's what I want you to tell me.''

''But you know, don't you? Or at least you suspect.''

''It doesn't matter what I suspect, Erin. You build a case on facts. You tell me what you know about the remains, and I'll take it from there.''

You do your job, Dr. Casey, and I'll do mine.

They both fell silent for a few minutes. The only sound was the rain on the roof and the crackle of the fire. Any other time, under any other circumstances, Erin would have found the cabin cozy, the setting romantic. Here she was, stranded with a handsome, sexy cop and she couldn't enjoy the moment because she had to worry about a murderer. Talk about bad luck.

''It's possible neither Clive Avery nor Jamie was the leak,'' she said after a bit. ''We could have been followed out here yesterday morning.''

Nick glanced at her. ''What makes you think that?''

''Because you came to my lab yesterday. You were noticed.''

She saw him frown in the firelight. ''By whom?''

''My secretary for one. A colleague of mine for another. And I have a feeling the dean of Hillsboro might know, too. He was trying to push me into talking about my cases to Ed Dawson last night.''

Nick's scowl deepened. ''Ed Dawson? You mean the superintendent of CPD was at that party you went to?''

Erin paused. ''I figured you already knew that.''

"Why would I know what Ed Dawson does in his spare time?"

"Because," she said, "he was there with your mother."

IF SHE'D SLAPPED HIM across the face, Nick couldn't have been more stunned. He stared at her for a long moment, the glimmer of firelight in her hair barely registering with him as he tried to convince himself she couldn't have said what he thought she said.

"No way. It couldn't have been my mother."

Erin shrugged again. "Maybe it wasn't. I just assumed she was your mother because her name was Gallagher and because she looked an awful lot like you. Especially her eyes..." She seemed to drift off, then caught herself. "And because she said she had a son who was a CPD detective. Three sons, as a matter-of fact."

"What did she look like?" he almost snapped.

"In her fifties, pretty. Dark hair. Very nice. Oh, and she said her name was Maggie."

Nick believed in coincidence as much as the next guy, but no way that description could fit anyone but his mother. But what the *hell* had she been doing with Ed Dawson? They knew each other from a long time ago. Dawson and Nick's father had been friends, not particularly close, but they'd had a beer, gone fishing now and then when Dawson and his family still lived in the old neighborhood. But the Dawsons had moved away just weeks after their daughter Ashley's brutal murder. And then Nick's father had disappeared while investigating her death.

After Daniel O'Roarke's conviction, Ed Dawson had then begun his campaign for the top spot on the police force, and the Gallaghers and the Dawsons stopped moving in the same social circles. Why Nick's mother would be at some stuffy college reception with Dawson, Nick couldn't figure. She hadn't dated since his father's disappearance. Hadn't even looked at another man.

So why now?

Eight years is a long time, a little voice reminded him.

Nick knew it shouldn't bother him that his mother might finally want to get on with her life. She was still young, still attractive. And if it had been anyone but Ed Dawson, anyone except a man who had been friends with Nick's father, anyone besides another cop...

If it had been any time except *now*.

But since the discovery of the bones, Nick's memories of his father had been so strong. At times, it was almost as if Nick could sense Sean Gallagher's presence, looking over his shoulder, guiding him to do the right thing.

Yesterday, he'd even imagined he'd seen his father on the Hillsboro campus, but that was impossible, of course, because his father was dead. Had been dead for eight years. Murdered by a man who might walk from prison in a few short weeks, unless Nick did something to stop it. And for that, he needed Erin's help.

She sat staring into the fire, her features soft and fragile in the flickering light. Her hair was still in a braid, but strands had come loose, curling about her face in long, shimmering tendrils. She reminded him of a painting he'd seen once at a museum—pale, innocent, with an almost mystical aura. But unmistakably woman.

Another time, under better circumstances, he would have leaned over and kissed her. He would have taken his time with her, tasting her delicate lips, loosening her hair until it fell wantonly down her back. He would have touched her all over, whispered to her what he wanted to do to her....

Assuming, of course, she hadn't slapped his face by that time.

He let the fantasy spin away with no small regret, and turned his attention back to the front door, to the darkness outside the cabin. A murderer was out there waiting, and since Nick had been the one to drag Erin into this mess, it was his duty to protect her, not to seduce her.

But it had been Nick's experience that one sometimes led almost inevitably to the other. He wondered if Erin was aware of that fact.

She glanced at him, her expression almost startled, and Nick had the uncanny notion that she had read his thoughts yet again.

"I almost forgot something," she said excitedly.

"What?"

"Ross Calvert, my research assistant, told me yesterday that he'd seen a man, a stranger, lurking outside the FAHIL building, pretending to read a book. When I came out, the man watched me for a while, then he got in his car and drove away. Ross was worried the man was following me for some reason, but what if he wasn't there because of me? What if he was following you?"

"Why didn't you tell me this before?"

"I'd forgotten about it," Erin said. "And besides, I didn't really think there was anything to it until now."

"But even if someone followed us out here from

Chicago,'' Nick said, ''that someone had to have been
tipped off about the remains. He knew what we were
doing and he came prepared, which means that any
way you want to slice it, there had to have been a leak
in Roy's office.''

Erin turned so that she could glance at Roy Glass.
''How well do you know him?''

''I've known him for years,'' Nick said. ''He and
my father used to be fishing buddies. They went back
a long way.''

''You trust him?''

''Yes. Roy's not the leak,'' Nick said firmly. ''I'd
stake my life on that.''

Erin gave him a sidelong glance. ''I think we already
have.''

Chapter Seven

Erin started awake, her mind coming fully alert in an instant. When had she fallen asleep? She'd been certain she'd never close her eyes again, at least not until she and Nick got out of this cabin safely, but at some point, she'd drifted off, and she could tell she'd been sleeping deeply.

She lay curled up next to Nick, her head resting against his broad chest. His heart drummed a rhythm, deep and steady, against her ear. The sound was infinitely comforting. No wonder she'd been sleeping so soundly.

His arm was around her, and his fingers were in her hair. Erin lay completely still, pretending to sleep, as her body reacted inwardly to his touch. His fingers swept back a tendril from her neck, and Erin trembled, tried to pretend she was stirring in her sleep.

She didn't want Nick to know that she was awake. Didn't want him to take his hand from her hair, his arm from around her. She didn't want to have to remove herself from his chest, and so Erin lay there with her eyes closed, and she sighed softly, dreamily to herself, thinking how nice it was not to be alone.

After a while, she felt a little guilty for the charade,

so she roused herself, stretching, and Nick's arm instantly disappeared from around her. Erin glanced up at him. "How long have I been asleep?"

"An hour, maybe. It's nearly dawn."

It was cold in the cabin. The fire had died down while she slept, and now Erin sat up stiffly, rubbing her hands up and down her arms. "How's Roy?"

They both glanced toward the silent figure on the couch. "I checked on him after you fell asleep," Nick said. "His breathing sounds a little stronger."

If he'd checked on Roy after she'd fallen asleep, then how had she ended up curled against him, practically in his arms? Had he put her there, or had she moved in her sleep, unconsciously acting out her dreams?

Feeling awkward, Erin got to her feet and went over to check Roy's pulse. Nick was right. The sheriff did seem better this morning, but if they didn't get him to a doctor soon, he could still be in serious trouble.

She glanced at Nick. He was up and about, too, busying himself with the fire. He rubbed his hand against his beard, as if realizing how badly he needed a shave.

She could do with a bit of freshening up herself, Erin thought, and excused herself to retreat to the bathroom to brush her teeth and wash her face.

When she came out, Nick was standing at the door. He opened it a crack and was gazing out into the growing daylight. In the distance, Erin heard the low drone of an engine, and her heart started to race. Daybreak had blunted the terrors of the night, but at the sound of the car engine moving steadily toward them, the danger came rushing back to her. She moved quickly to Nick's side.

"What is it?"

"Four-wheel drive trucks, I'd guess. More than one, by the sounds of it," he said without looking at her. "Get back in the cabin and stay down."

Erin wasn't the type to stand around asking foolish questions or challenging authority in the face of danger. She was the master in her lab, but in this situation, Nick was the expert, and she didn't hesitate for a moment to do as he said. She hurried over to the fireplace and picked up Roy Glass's gun.

The roar of the engines grew louder, masking the sound of her own heartbeat in her ears. She kept her eyes on Nick's back, taking comfort in the knowledge that he had kept them alive thus far.

The engines were cut suddenly, and Nick said over his shoulder, "Stay down."

Erin knelt at the end of the couch as she clutched the weapon in trembling hands. After a few moments, she heard someone shout over a bullhorn, "I'm Deputy Selworth with the Webber County Sheriff's Department. Anyone in there?"

Nick said from the doorway, "I'm Detective Nick Gallagher from the Chicago Police Department. Move forward slowly and let me see your hands."

"We're going to have to ask you to put down your weapon, Detective Gallagher," came back the response over the bullhorn.

"Not until I see some ID," Nick shouted.

Silence, as if the men outside were conferring with someone else, then another voice came over the bullhorn. "This is Jamie Duncan, Detective. These men are from the sheriff's office. I can vouch for that. I went for help last night after I found Clive's body."

"I'm still going to need to see their ID," Nick informed them coolly. "You can bring them to me, Jamie."

Another silence. Erin held her breath. After a few moments, footsteps bounded up the porch steps and she heard Jamie's voice. "It's okay, Detective. You can trust these men."

He handed the wallet IDs to Nick, who scanned the names and pictures. Satisfied, he gave them back to Jamie. "What happened to you last night?"

"I heard a noise and went out to investigate. I didn't want to awaken the rest of you because I thought it might not be anything more than a deer. But then I saw footprints in the mud, I followed the tracks, and next thing I knew, Clive was dead."

"So you bolted?" Nick said coldly.

Erin could almost see the young deputy's blush. "I knew we needed help. I figured I cut could through the woods to high ground, make it out to the highway or a farmhouse and call the station for backup."

He sounded sincere, and Erin was inclined to believe him, but Nick was more cautious. "I've got Sheriff Glass inside here. He's hurt pretty badly. We're going to need to get him to a hospital."

"We've got an ambulance waiting at the highway," Jamie said. "The water's gone down, but we'll have to use the four-wheel drives to get back to the main road."

Over the bullhorn, one of the deputies said, "We've put away our weapons, Detective Gallagher. We're coming up to the porch."

Nick opened the door and stepped out. Erin got cautiously to her feet and moved across the room to the door, staying out of sight but determined to cover Nick's back, if need be.

He and the police officers conversed in low tones for several minutes, then they all came inside. Erin let the weapon fall to her side as her gaze met Nick's and he nodded briefly.

Within minutes, Sheriff Glass had been secured to a portable stretcher and transported to one of the trucks. Nick and Erin climbed into the other one.

Nick squeezed her hand. "You okay?"

She nodded and let out a long breath.

"You did good," he said, and the look he gave her made Erin's heart race even faster.

IT WAS LATE afternoon by the time Erin and Nick were able to return to Chicago. The bones were stored in the FAHIL lab under tight security, awaiting Erin's preliminary examination first thing the next morning. For now, however, all she wanted was a hot bath and a good night's sleep.

Nick walked her up the stairs to her apartment. The evening had grown chilly with a stiff wind blowing in from the lake. Erin shivered as she unlocked her door.

"What a trip," she said with some irony.

He stared down at her in the fading light. "Are you going to be okay here tonight?"

She grimaced. "I'm so exhausted right now the ceiling could cave in on me and I wouldn't know it."

"You've got an alarm system?" When she nodded, he said, "Then be sure to turn it on."

His words sent a shiver racing through her, reminding her of the danger they'd faced just a few short hours ago. "Don't worry. I will."

"See you in the morning, then."

He started toward the stairs, but Erin said softly, "Nick?"

He turned back. "Yes."

She hesitated then shrugged.

He gazed down at her, his blue eyes almost electric in the dying light. His face was shadowed, tense. And then he smiled. "Just Nick?"

Her heart rolled inside her chest. "Thanks for…you know…everything."

"You don't need to thank me. If it wasn't for me, you wouldn't even have been there last night."

True enough, but in spite of everything that had happened, Erin couldn't muster up even a glimmer of regret. She was sorry Clive Avery had been killed, sorry that Sheriff Glass was injured, but she wasn't the least bit sorry that she had spent the night with Nick Gallagher, or that the danger had created an intimacy between them that might otherwise never have developed.

This time, as he gazed down at her, it was almost as if he'd read her mind. Before she had time to catch her breath, he bent and brushed his lips against hers.

And then he was gone.

TOO RESTLESS to sleep, Nick decided to head over to the station and get caught up on some paperwork—the curse of a cop's existence. But as he sat in his cubicle, trying to focus on his current caseload, his mind raced elsewhere.

Clive Avery's murder troubled him. Nick had wanted to keep the discovery of the remains and the excavation as quiet as possible until he knew what he was dealing with—in other words, until he found out whether or not the remains were his father's. Nor had he wanted to reveal his findings prematurely to the media or to the O'Roarkes. Let them think Daniel was about to walk from prison. Let them be so preoccupied with their victory celebration they wouldn't stop to think that if Sean Gallagher's body ever surfaced, it could mean another conviction for Daniel.

But somehow, the O'Roarkes *had* found out about the remains. Who else would be desperate enough to commit murder in order to keep the identity of the skeleton a secret?

"Hey, Nick, what are you doing here this time of night?"

Nick glanced up to find his uncle standing in the doorway of his cubicle. The squad room outside was noisy, as usual, and he hadn't heard his uncle approach. A seasoned detective in the twilight of his career, Liam Gallagher, with his white hair and piercing blue eyes, was still a man to be reckoned with. He'd started in law enforcement nearly forty years ago, walking the same beat on the far south side as his father had walked before him and his brother, Sean, had after him. He was the eldest Gallagher on the force now, which gave him a certain freedom in doling out unsolicited advice.

Nick braced himself. "Looks like you're burning the midnight oil yourself."

Liam shrugged as he came into Nick's office and sat down heavily. He would be retiring in a couple more years, and Nick thought that his uncle suddenly looked as if he was ready for it. The lines in his face had deepened over the last few years, and the slump in his shoulders was now permanent. "Lot of uncleared cases, but what else is new? Number of detectives is down while the murder rate continues to climb."

Actually, the crime rate nationwide was down, but Nick didn't point that out to his uncle. "So, what's on your mind?" he asked casually.

"I noticed you took a few days off this week." Liam eyed him shrewdly.

Nick leaned back in his chair and stretched. "I had the time coming."

"I know you did. I'm not complaining. Just wondered where you'd gone off to. Do a little fishing?"

Something in his uncle's voice set off an alarm inside Nick. He shook his head. "I don't fish much these days."

"Too bad. When you were a kid, I seem to recall that's all you wanted to do."

Nick's father had been alive then. It wasn't the fishing Nick had enjoyed so much as the time he and Sean had spent together. "It's not the same anymore."

"Yeah, I know." Liam didn't say anything else, but somehow Nick knew they were both thinking about Sean. He and Liam had always been close, closer than Nick was to either of his brothers, he thought with regret.

"So, what's up?" he asked, knowing that something was on his uncle's mind. Liam Gallagher didn't make small talk just for the hell of it.

Liam stared at him for a moment, a long, probing gaze. "I got a call today from a buddy of mine in Webber County, Wisconsin. He said the sheriff over there was pretty seriously wounded last night, and one of his deputies was killed. They were ambushed in the woods near Sean's fishing cabin. You wouldn't know anything about that incident, would you, Nick?"

Nick returned his uncle's glare without flinching. "Why would you think I'd know anything about it?"

"Because you and Roy Glass have become good friends over the years. And because I know you still go up there from time to time, looking for Sean's body.

You've found him this time, haven't you? Or at least, you think you have.''

Nick scrubbed a hand across his eyes. He was suddenly exhausted. "How did you know?"

"I know Roy Glass, too. I used to go fishing with him and Sean. He called and told me about the remains right after he called you. Then you hightailed it up there so quick I didn't have time to talk to you, and you almost got yourself killed in the process. Nice job, Nick.''

His tone rubbed Nick the wrong way. "So, what would you have had me do? Leave him up there until I could go through the proper channels and in the meantime, give the O'Roarkes time to destroy the evidence? In case you haven't figured it out, they somehow found out about the remains, too. They're responsible for Clive Avery's murder.''

"I don't doubt it. But you should have come to me," Liam said angrily. "I would have helped you, and that deputy might still be alive.''

Nick grimaced. He'd thought about that himself. Maybe he should have called in reinforcements, but, hell, hindsight was always twenty-twenty. "Look, it's done now. The remains are at FAHIL. They'll be examined by a highly competent forensic anthropologist. When we know what we're dealing with, we can go from there.''

Liam gave him a hard look. "You mean when you learn whether or not the remains belong to Sean. So, what if they don't, Nick?''

"What do you mean?''

"If the remains aren't Sean's, where do you go from there? You've waited a long time for your revenge.''

Nick said coldly, "You call it revenge, I call it justice."

"Call it whatever you like," Liam said. "It still boils down to the same thing. You want to get the O'Roarkes. Hell, I can understand that. I feel the same way. I got no use for the whole damned lot of them, never have had, and Kaitlin's marrying one of the bastards didn't change my mind one bit." He paused, no doubt reflecting on his daughter's union to Dylan O'Roarke, Daniel's cousin. In a way, Kaitlin and Dylan's marriage had been the ultimate revenge by the O'Roarkes. Liam had disowned his daughter, which had caused the whole family untold grief.

Nick's anger evaporated at his uncle. He said wearily, "All I want is for Daniel O'Roarke to get what he deserves. If that takes proving he killed my father, then so be it."

"Eight years is a long time," Liam warned. "The trail's cold by now, Nick. The evidence long gone. Proving he killed Sean won't be easy."

"I never said it would be. But I'm willing to bet that in all these years, Daniel O'Roarke has talked to someone in prison, bragged about wasting a cop, about where he left the body or the murder weapon. *Something.* The evidence is there somewhere. I just have to find it."

"And if you don't?"

"I will." Nick wouldn't entertain the notion of failure. Not now. Not after all these years. Not when a cold-blooded murderer could go free. He stared at his uncle for a moment, seeing his father's face instead. "I'm a cop, for God's sake. If I can't bring my own father's killer to justice, then what does that say about me?"

"Maybe it says you're human," Liam said gruffly. "Just like the rest of us."

AFTER THE EXCITEMENT and danger, and, yes, the thrill, of the past two days, Erin's apartment seemed even quieter than normal. Macavity was happy to see her for about two minutes, but then he stalked off to sulk in his favorite corner, staring at her through baleful, green eyes.

"I'm sorry, Mac, but I was stranded," Erin tried to explain to the black-and-white feline. "I couldn't get back."

Yes, but did you even want to get back? a little voice whispered accusingly. Because in spite of the danger and fear, Erin had never felt more alive—and less alone—than she had in Nick Gallagher's company.

As if reading her mind, Macavity turned in an unforgiving huff to clean his front paws, ignoring Erin completely and making her realize again just how fickle a companion a cat could be.

Suddenly, Erin missed her mother more than she could bear, and she wished that she could pick up the phone and call her, tell her all about her new job and the harrowing adventure she'd just experienced.

But Erin especially longed to talk to her mother about Nick, about the possibility that she might be falling for him.

"What you need is a good, long soak," Erin told herself aloud, letting her voice fill some of the emptiness of the apartment.

A hot bath had been her mother's cure-all for everything from heartbreak to hangnails, but the remedy didn't work tonight. The longer Erin stayed in the tub, the more tense she became. No matter how hard she tried, she couldn't relax, nor could she dispel the dread hovering over her like a thundercloud.

The remains that had been uncovered—that were even now awaiting her in the lab—were like a Pandora's box. An evil had been unleashed upon the discovery of the bones, and Erin knew that she had been irrevocably drawn into the maelstrom. Even before she'd gone to the cabin, she'd sensed trouble, some dark underbelly that, once exposed, could defile her in ways she didn't yet understand.

Telling herself she was being overly dramatic, not to mention paranoid, Erin tried to turn her thoughts from the danger and concentrate instead on the memory of Nick's kiss, the butterfly graze of his lips against hers. She shivered in the tepid water, lifting her fingers to her mouth, circling her lips the way she imagined Nick doing it. The water lapped against her skin, touching her intimately, making her want Nick in a way she'd never before longed for a man.

And yet even in her yearning, even in the heat of her attraction, Erin knew there was something taboo about Nick Gallagher. That they were conferring on a case was the least of it. When she looked at him, she experienced a sense of foreboding that was almost as deep and almost as basic as her desire for him. She wondered if there could be one without the other—if the secrets she sensed in him drew her to him. If her desire for him made her fear him.

Climbing out of the tub, she dried off, then pulled on a pair of pajamas and crawled into bed. She lay for a long time, drowsy, her thoughts sporadic until a sound outside her apartment brought her upright in bed. Macavity, having graciously decided to forgive her after all, was curled at the foot of her bed, his ears back, his eyes wide and glowing in the darkness. He'd heard something, too.

Her heart pounding, Erin got out of bed and slipped through the darkened apartment, pausing every few seconds to listen for the noise. Her living room window looked down on her landlady's backyard, a maze of flower beds and shrubs, shaded by a thick awning of leaves. Tree limbs tossed in the darkness, and the sound came to Erin again, faintly at first, and then stronger, as the breeze stiffened. Wind chimes clanked together in the wind, the sound too metallic to be musical. Erin had heard the chimes before and never been bothered by them, but tonight her nerves were frail, whether she wanted to admit it or not.

Turning away from the window, she walked around the bar that separated the living area of her apartment from the tiny, L-shaped kitchen. She got down a glass, poured herself a drink from the faucet, and as she stood sipping the water, she glanced out the window. The kitchen window looked out on the street, and her gaze was instantly drawn to a long, black car parked at the curb.

It was sitting across the street from her apartment, out of the glow of the streetlight. She could barely make out the lines of the car, but Erin had the impression of sleekness, of a panther crouching in the darkness. As she stood peering through the shadows, a movement at the rear of the car caught her attention. Again she had only an impression, but Erin thought she saw the glint of reflected light on glass as the rear window lowered. And then the unmistakable sensation of eyes staring at her through the darkness.

Chapter Eight

"The remains are definitely male." Erin brushed her fingers gently across the prominent brow ridge, the sloping forehead, focusing her attention on the skeleton and not on Nick, who stood across the worktable from her. On the fact that her heart was pounding like a jackhammer at his nearness. She'd been wanting to see him all day, but he'd waited until late afternoon before stopping by the lab to hear her preliminary report.

"See the horizontal teardrop shape of the eye orbits and the tall, narrow nasal opening? That tells us the remains are Caucasoid."

"A white male," he summarized. "Go on."

"Look at the color of the bones. The ivory finish and smooth texture have eroded, and the grayish color is a sign that the bones have been exposed on the ground's surface for quite some time, five years at least."

Their gazes met again, but this time, he didn't comment. Erin couldn't tell if he was pleased by her findings or not. He was very stoic, almost aloof, and she was beginning to wonder whether she'd imagined the brief kiss he'd given her last night. Today, he seemed hardly aware of her.

"I've used several markers to put his age at somewhere between fifty and sixty. There're signs of arthritis at the joints and the spine, but no heavy pitting in the surface of the auricular region of the hip bone, which suggests an age a little younger than sixty." Should she explain in more detail or was he willing to take her word for it?

When he didn't challenge her, she continued. "Height, around six-two. Weight, 190 to 220, but weight is a lot more difficult to determine than height or age. Fat doesn't leaving markings on bone. However, there are formulas we use depending on the skeleton's frame, the person's sex and height and muscle attachment markings. The more a person uses a muscle, the rougher the bone's surface becomes in order to anchor the tendons." She showed him what she meant. "I'd say this man was in reasonably good shape for his age, probably even worked out. And he was right-handed."

Nick was gazing at her, not the skeleton. His expression looked grave. "Okay," he said almost tersely. "Let's cut to the chase, then. Cause and manner of death?"

"Undetermined."

He sucked in his breath. "You're sure?"

Erin nodded. "Undetermined as of now. The radiographs didn't show any traces of metal, nor was there evidence of an entry or exit wound. I've pretty much eliminated death by gunshot. There is, however, a small fracture on the back of the skull." She turned the skull over to show him the wound. "The X rays showed that the fracture was perimortem. The bone was damaged before death, not after."

"He was hit in the back of the head," Nick said.

"Could be."

"Then why did you say that cause of death is undetermined?"

"Because, in my opinion, the trauma to the skull wasn't severe enough to cause death. But there's something else. There's a separation in the hyoid bone." She touched the center of her throat.

"Which means?"

"The hyoid is a bone in the throat that anchors the tongue. It can be damaged or broken during strangulation."

His gaze was riveted on her now. "And this man's hyoid was broken?"

"Maybe. The hyoid starts out in three pieces—the U-shaped center and two horns. By a person's mid-thirties, the horns usually fuse to the body of the hyoid, but sometimes they don't. In other words, the break may not be a break at all, but perfectly natural for this individual. I'll have to study the bone more thoroughly before I can make that determination."

"But you haven't ruled out the possibility of a violent death." Nick's voice was low and urgent. His gaze on her deepened. Suddenly, he was no longer aloof, but focused and passionate. A man with a single-minded purpose. Erin wished she knew what that purpose was.

She met his gaze steadily. "Quite the contrary. If I were a betting woman, I'm afraid I'd have to put my money on murder at this point."

ERIN LOCKED UP the lab and then set the alarm before she and Nick left the building a little while later. They stood on the steps outside, talking softly for a moment about the case.

"You understand this is only my preliminary analysis. I'll need to do a much more in-depth examination, and then I'll need you, or someone, to bring me a list of missing persons who disappeared from that area in the last, say, five to ten years. If we don't get any matches from that, we'll broaden the search. We may eventually want to look at missing persons from the Chicago area for that time period."

"What about a cast reconstruction of the victim's face?" Nick asked her.

"That's usually a last resort, but it can sometimes help."

"I read about a case once where a clay reconstruction of a murder victim's face was allowed to be present in the courtroom during the trial. Afterward, some of the jurors said that when they stared at the model, they had an eerie feeling the real murder victim was staring back at them."

Erin glanced up at him. "Did they convict the defendant?"

"In less than an hour."

"Is that why you want a clay reconstruction of 00-04?" she asked carefully.

His gaze hardened. "If it would help, you bet. I'd do just about anything to put a murderer where he belongs."

Twilight fell over the campus, and the wind picked up, stirring the trees and sending a chill up Erin's backbone. She stared up at Nick, thinking how complex her life had become since he'd first walked into her lab. She could have been murdered herself in that cabin, and even now, back in her own element, she was being drawn irrevocably into the web he was spinning, the trap he was laying for someone. Could she break free, if she chose to?

She had a feeling it was too late for that. Had been too late the moment he came into her lab.

"Have you had dinner yet?" he asked suddenly.

She shook her head.

"You like Chinese? I know this great little place in Chinatown."

"I love Chinese," she said, feeling the gossamer strands of his web tightening around her, but she knew, instinctively, that struggling would do her no good.

What could she do but let the inevitable happen?

NICK DROVE Erin home to change, and when they were again settled in his car, he glanced at her appreciatively. She wore jeans and a light-blue sweater set that matched her eyes and made her look very feminine. She'd rebraided her hair, and he had to fight the urge to tug loose the band that held the strands together. He'd only seen her with her hair down once, but it was a sight he hadn't been able to forget. He'd fantasized about that hair, dreamed about it.

With grim resolve, he nosed the car away from the curb and glanced in his rearview mirror. Half a block back, a dark-colored sedan pulled out behind them.

"Have you checked on Roy Glass's condition today?" Erin asked him.

"I drove back up there this morning. He regained consciousness overnight. The doctors say he's going to be okay, but he doesn't remember much about the night before. He didn't see who attacked him."

"Did they find Avery's body?"

"Not yet. Not much in the way of trace evidence, either. The rain took care of that." Nick watched his mirror. The black car was still behind them, hanging back, every once in a while letting another car get between them. But Nick knew a tail when he saw one. He accelerated slightly.

He wondered if he was making a mistake, still not calling in reinforcements. But he wasn't ready to make public the discovery of the remains, not until Erin's findings were conclusive. A media onslaught was the last thing he needed. Luckily, Clive Avery's murder hadn't been reported by either of the major Chicago papers. A small-town homicide didn't carry much weight in the big city.

"It's hard to believe that forty-eight hours ago our lives were in danger," Erin said. "We could have been killed." Her tone was almost matter-of-fact, as if the shock and fear were already starting to fade.

Nick said darkly, "The threat is still there, Erin. Don't get careless."

She glanced at him in alarm. "What do you mean?"

"Why would someone take the kind of risks the killer took at the cabin just to disappear once we brought the remains back to Chicago?"

"You're saying the murderer followed us back here?"

"His actions back at the cabin prove how desperate he is. He was willing to kill every one of us to keep the identity of that skeleton a secret." Nick glanced at her, saw her shiver.

"There was this case in Knoxville just before I left," she said. "We had to recover the remains of three men who had been shot to death and buried in one grave. We got word that the men had been killed in a drug deal that went sour, and that a drug lord from Miami was keeping tabs on our excavation work. The state police were called out to guard us while we worked. The situation was pretty tense.''

''What happened?''

''We completed our work and took the remains back to the lab. The three dead men were identified, but as far as I know, an arrest was never made in the case. But for a while, I thought someone was following me. I learned to take precautions.''

''Like the security system in the lab and at your apartment?''

She nodded.

''Is that why you know how to use a gun?''

She hesitated, turning to stare out the side window for a moment. ''That came before, when I was still in college. Our house was broken into once and ransacked. The local police seemed to think it was vandals, since nothing valuable was taken. But it scared my mother pretty badly. She and I lived alone, so she insisted that we both learn how to defend ourselves.''

''Not a bad idea,'' Nick said. The black car behind them turned left, disappearing into traffic. ''Does your mother still live in Knoxville?''

She turned to face him. ''She died last year.''

''I'm sorry.'' Nick wanted to reach out and take her hand, tell her he understood such a loss, but instead, he gripped the steering wheel tighter. ''My father died a long time ago. I wish I could tell you it gets easier.''

''But it doesn't. I already know that. Were you and your father close?'' she asked almost wistfully.

''Yeah.'' Of the three boys, Nick was the one closest to his father. John had always been fiercely independent, Tony a loner. Neither one of them had spent as much time with Sean as Nick had. He'd enjoyed the fishing weekends he and his father had spent at the cabin, the camaraderie they'd shared while watching a Bears game on TV. Nick had genuinely liked his father's company, and sometimes he felt he hadn't had a close friend, someone he could really count on, since his father's disappearance.

He felt Erin's hand on his arm, and he glanced at her. She smiled. "It doesn't get any easier, but we do move on, don't we? Life's too short to live in the past."

Nick *had* moved on. He'd lived his life. Over the years, there'd been days, weeks, even months when he hadn't even thought of his father's disappearance. But it was always there, lingering in the back of his mind, a wound that had healed over cleanly enough, but remained tender.

But the threat of Daniel O'Roarke's release had opened everything up. Nick had learned to live with his father's death, even accept it, but he could not live with the idea of his father's murderer going free.

He found a parking place, and the two of them got out to walk down the street to the restaurant. Chinatown at night was always intriguing with its tiny, exotic shops, crowded restaurants, and colorful, towering pagodas.

The evening was cool and clear, the kind of night that always gave Nick a nostalgic tug for the years growing up with his brothers, when they'd been closer. After their father's disappearance, whatever innocence that remained of their childhood had also vanished, and the family had never been the same.

They'd each handled their grief in their own way, but they hadn't turned to one another. John had tried to become the caretaker of the family, which had grated on his own independence, and Tony had gone in the opposite direction. He'd pulled away from the family altogether, and was only now, eight years later, finding his way back.

As for Nick…his grief had turned into anger, a slow, festering rage that had been brought to a dangerous level by the prospect of Daniel O'Roarke's release. If he couldn't prove O'Roarke had murdered his father…if O'Roarke did walk from prison…

Nick suppressed a shudder, not wanting to contemplate what might happen if he someday met Daniel O'Roarke on the street. Maybe his uncle had been right. Maybe what Nick sought was revenge.

Erin wasn't touching him as they walked along the narrow street, but suddenly, her presence filled his senses, more keenly than if she'd taken his arm or touched his shoulder. His steps slowed, and he stood for a moment, gazing down at her.

There was something about her he couldn't define. An attraction, yes, but something more. Something deeper. Something that stirred feelings in him he didn't quite welcome. He was on a mission, he reminded himself, and he didn't have time for romance.

But Erin Casey was a very romantic woman. That was the only way he knew to describe her. She wasn't as beautiful or openly sexy as some women he'd known, but sensual and secretive, her clear blue eyes like alluring pools with hidden depths. Nick was drawn to her in a way he couldn't ever remember being drawn to anyone else. And that was a very dangerous thing for him.

"Something wrong?" she asked in her soft, Southern drawl.

He shook his head slightly, as if to clear his thoughts. "I was just thinking how much I'd like to…"

When he trailed off, she cocked her head. "What?"

Slowly he lifted his hand and drew his knuckles across her cheek. *Like silk,* he thought. Just as he knew it would be.

He sensed more than saw her tremble at his touch, and a powerful urge rose inside him. He didn't much care that they were standing on a public street, that passersby were already staring at them curiously. Nick had never been an openly demonstrative man, but Erin brought out a tenderness in him he'd never known he possessed.

Almost at once, he dropped his hand to his side. "Maybe we should go eat," he said softly.

She nodded, but her smile seemed disappointed. "Maybe we should," she agreed.

Within minutes they were seated in a booth, a candle flickering between them as they studied the menus and then placed their orders.

Nick watched Erin in the candlelight. The soft light flattered her features, making her skin seem even smoother, her eyes even bluer. Making him wanting to kiss her even more than he had outside.

"I've been thinking about Clive Avery," she said suddenly.

Not exactly the topic on Nick's mind. "What about him?"

She hesitated, as if unwilling to speak ill of the dead. "There was something about him I didn't trust. I'm usually a pretty good judge of character, and I knew from the first there was something…odd about him. When I saw him talking on his cell phone, I could tell he didn't want me overhearing any of the conversation. Then in the woods—" She broke off, looking uncomfortable.

"He hit on you, didn't he?"

She frowned slightly. "How did you know?"

"I know his type." Nick could imagine the scenario in the woods. Avery, accustomed to having women fall all over him, made a pass and Erin turned him down. He wouldn't like taking no for an answer. He might even have gotten physical. Nick felt the heat of anger as he glanced at Erin protectively.

Easy, a voice told him. *The man's dead, remember?*

Besides, it was obvious Erin could take care of herself.

"What happened?" he asked her.

"Nothing much. But he kept asking me about the remains, insisting that you must have told me something about the victim's identity."

Nick didn't much like the sound of that. "I've ordered a background check on both Avery and Jamie Duncan."

She glanced at him in surprise. "Isn't that a little out of your jurisdiction?"

He shrugged without answering. John was the one caught up on rules. Tony was the one who always broke them. Nick fell somewhere in the middle. If there'd been a leak in Roy Glass's office that had almost gotten them all killed, then Nick was damn well going to find it. He didn't care whose toes he stepped on.

Their food came then, and they ate mostly in silence, making the occasional comment about the spicy dishes, the wine, and later, reciting aloud their fortunes.

"Beware of tall, dark strangers," Erin read, and Nick saw her blush in the candlelight.

"Beware of small, brilliant anthropologists," he ad-libbed.

"It doesn't say that." She made a grab for his fortune, but he held it just out of her reach. When the waiter came to collect his credit card, Nick laid the strip of paper on the table to fish out his wallet. Erin picked it up.

You will find love when and where you least expect it.

Their gazes met in the candlelight. Nick could have sworn he saw something that might have been desire swirling in the depths of those beguiling blue eyes. Or was he only seeing what he wanted to see?

DRIVING HOME, Nick kept an eye on his rearview mirror, but the black car didn't appear again, and if another tail had picked them up, he couldn't spot it.

He pulled to the curb in front of Erin's apartment and shut off the engine. The silence between them grew awkward. It was as if they were both aware of the attraction between them, but neither was willing to admit it, let alone act upon it. Nick wasn't at all sure he was Erin's type. Maybe she liked brainier men. Academics. What did a cop have to offer someone like her?

But her soft gaze told him the exact opposite. She did like him. She did want him. All he had to do was lean over and kiss her.

"Thank you for dinner," she said breathlessly, as if sensing his intention. "It was lovely."

He leaned an arm on the steering wheel as he turned to face her. "Least I could do after everything you're doing for me."

"I'm just doing my job."

"I'm glad you're the one who's doing it."

"Nick..." She glanced at him, the question on her

lips dying before she spoke it. She gave a tiny shrug and smiled. "Good night."

But when she would have opened the door, he took her hand, tugging gently until she turned back around to face him. Their gazes clung in the darkness, and then Nick reached up to touch a stray curl at her temple.

Erin's eyes fluttered closed and he thought he saw her tremble. Was she nervous, or excited? Maybe a little of both, as he was. He'd never known a woman quite like her. She was intelligent, attractive, extremely competent and highly respected, but there was also an air of innocence about her. A vulnerability that made him hesitate to do or say anything that might cause her future pain.

But it was too late for that. The danger in the cabin had drawn them together, bonded them, and the lingering threat kept them allies. He reached for her, and she came hesitantly, as if she'd been racked with the same self-doubts as he. But the moment his lips touched hers, Nick's qualms faded. He didn't much care what the future held then. All he cared about was here and now, with Erin trembling and pliant in his arms, her delectable body straining toward his.

THEY WERE still kissing. They'd been kissing for the longest time. Erin felt like a teenager, breathless and excited, a little bit naughty.

Actually, this was the way she'd imagined she would have felt if she'd gone parking with the high school hunk. In reality, such a guy had never looked at her twice…until now.

That a man like Nick Gallagher found her attractive, wanted her…

His mouth, firm and insistent on hers, told her just

how much he did want her. He tasted faintly of wine, a rich, ambrosial tang that sent Erin's head spinning. She opened her mouth to his, and sensed his surprise at her submission. Then, with a low groan, he captured her face in his hands, weaving his fingers through her hair as the heat between them began to rise in slow, undulating waves. He deepened the kiss with his tongue, tasting, exploring, savoring until Erin felt all weak and quivery inside.

Lois was right, she thought. Nick would be an incredible lover.

Even kissing her, he was so utterly, completely, wonderfully masterful. Just as Erin knew he would be. Just as she'd hoped he would be.

Beware of tall, dark strangers…

She pushed the warning from her mind, sighing deeply as she leaned back in the seat and pressed her hands against his chest. Her fingers slid inside his shirt, feeling warm, hard skin and the erotic beat of his heart. Her own heartbeat went crazy.

The night was cool and breezy, but the interior of Nick's car grew steamy. Hardly breaking the kiss, he shifted, pulling her across his lap, placing her legs on either side of him so that their bodies were touching intimately. Dangerously. Thrill after thrill snaked up Erin's spine as she felt Nick's hands inside her sweater, then tugging at the snap of her jeans.

They were going a little too fast, and as Erin pulled back to catch her breath, her elbow hit the horn. The unexpected sound blasted them apart.

Nick looked as dazed as Erin felt. "Damn," he murmured.

His shaken tone expressed her sentiments exactly. It had been a few very earth-shattering moments.

He glanced around, as if he'd completely lost track of his surroundings. "Damn," he said again, more forcefully this time.

Erin still didn't say anything. She scrambled out of his lap, back to her own seat. In the aftermath of such passion, she was experiencing no small amount of embarrassment. She couldn't believe she'd let herself lose control like that, here, on a public street, with a man she hardly knew. In another moment, she might have been ripping off his clothes.

Damn...

She cleared her throat. "It's getting late. I should go in."

"Maybe you'd better."

They got out of the car, and he walked her up the steps to her apartment. Erin turned after unlocking her door, marveling at how far they'd come since the chaste kiss he'd given her last night.

Beware of tall, dark strangers...

The fortune was like a mantra inside her head. Her heart was still hammering, and as Erin gazed up at Nick, she realized that in spite of her embarrassment, in spite of her reserve, in spite of that stupid fortune, she wanted him to kiss her again, not chastely. She wanted him to carry her inside, lay her on the bed and make love to her all night long.

Which was not at all like her.

Since the first time her heart had been broken in college, she didn't usually react impulsively to men she was attracted to. The lesson she'd learned had been far too bitter, but with Nick...Nick was different. Nick wasn't just an attraction. She liked and admired him, and with very little effort, she could let herself fall in love with him.

Which was not at all like her.

But as she bid Nick good-night and let herself in the door, Erin had the disturbing notion that perhaps she didn't know herself quite as well as she'd once thought. Perhaps her fortune should have read, *Beware of the stranger within.*

NICK LET HIMSELF into his apartment a little while later, switched on a light, and threw his car keys onto a table near the front door, where he could find them in a hurry if he needed them. A haunting remnant of Erin's perfume, something surprisingly dark and sensual, clung to his jacket. He shrugged it off, lifting the fabric to his nose for a moment before tossing it toward the closet.

This wasn't good, he decided. This wasn't at all good. The timing was all wrong. He wasn't looking for an affair, let alone a relationship. But tonight he'd almost started both with Erin.

He was surprised how quickly she'd gotten under his skin. What was it about her that made him think of her before he fell asleep each night, that made him dream about her? What was it about her that made him want her in a way he'd never before wanted a woman? And the hell of it was, she wasn't right for him. What could they possibly have in common? Except, of course, for that kiss...

He strode into the kitchen and got himself a beer out of the refrigerator. That had been one great kiss, he had to admit. She might not be the most beautiful woman he'd ever known, or the sexiest in some respects, but she damn sure knew how to kiss. It made him wonder what else she'd be good at.

But the timing, he reminded himself again, was all

wrong. He had to concentrate on one thing and one thing only right now: proving Daniel O'Roarke had killed his father. Keeping the bastard in prison where he belonged.

Nick lay down on the sofa, placing his weapon and his beer within easy reach. Staring at the ceiling, he tried to think out his strategy, but his mind kept turning back to Erin. To that kiss. To the way she'd looked and felt and smelled.

You will find love when and where you least expect it.

Great, he thought almost miserably. That was the last thing he needed.

He got up, threw on his jacket, and headed outside. He didn't have a clue where he was going, but after awhile, he found himself pulling up outside the house where he'd grown up. The lights were out. His mother, sister and grandmother had long since gone to bed, and as Nick got out of his car, he closed the door gently, not wanting to rouse anyone.

He sat on the stoop, letting the lake wind sweep over him as memories of his father came rushing back. Sean, in a fishing boat, showing Nick how to bait a hook. In the front row at Nick's ball game, cheering him on. Taking him out for his first beer. Busting his chops over a speeding ticket. Sean, watching proudly, as Nick graduated from the police academy…

The memories were so sharp and clear that his father's presence was almost a tangible thing. Nick could even smell the sweet aroma of the cigars Sean had favored for special occasions, and for a moment, as the scent drifted on the wind, everything inside Nick stilled. He lifted his head, glancing around the darkened yard.

Next door, the neighbor's dog started barking, as if a stranger were nearby. The yapping rose to a crescendo, then stopped abruptly, as if the dog's fears had somehow been abated by a soft command, a pat on the head. His father had always loved dogs, Nick remembered, and they him.

The cigar smoke lingered faintly on the air, and the hair on the back of Nick's neck rose. "Dad?"

There was no answer, of course, because Sean Gallagher was dead.

Chapter Nine

Nick sat at his desk the next day, trying to make sense of the notes he'd written that morning. So far, nothing surprising had turned up in the background check he'd run on Jamie Duncan. As Nick suspected, the young deputy had been born and raised in Webber County, Wisconsin. His family still lived there, and his credentials, though somewhat limited, appeared solid.

Clive Avery, on the other hand, had turned out to be a little more intriguing. Before joining the Webber County Sheriff's Department seven years ago, Avery had lived in Chicago. He'd graduated from the police academy with top honors, and had served on the force for nearly five years before being dismissed. But when Nick had tried to call up the man's service record, he'd been denied access.

Interesting, to say the least. It was possible the explanation was as simple as Avery having a friend on the force who had done him a favor by making his record unavailable in order to protect him. But from what? Why had Avery been dismissed? And what, if anything, did that have to do with his murder?

Nick couldn't see a connection, unless Avery's path had somehow crossed with the O'Roarkes while he'd still been with CPD. Maybe he'd been on their payroll back then. God knew they owned enough cops, Nick thought bitterly.

Richard O'Roarke was a ruthless, brutal man—just like his son—and he would do anything, including ordering the murder of innocent people, to set Daniel free. The O'Roarkes had always taken care of each other, no matter who they had to hurt in the process, and Richard O'Roarke had very long arms. He was powerful enough to have bought off Clive Avery, and vicious enough to have him killed after he had given Richard what he wanted.

The thing that worried Nick the most about all this now was Erin. She was the key to his case, and her life could be in danger because of it. If Richard O'Roarke thought that Erin stood in the way of his son's freedom, he would as soon gun her down as look at her. Nick had to make sure he protected her. If anything happened to Erin because of him—

"Nick?"

He glanced up. His mother was standing in the doorway of his office, watching him quizzically. "You look as if you're a million miles away."

"I guess I was." He paused, trying to organize his thoughts as he stood. "What brings you to the station?"

She smiled, drawing her fingers through her short, dark curls. "Oh, I was in the area getting my hair done, so I thought I'd stop by and remind Liam about your grandmother's birthday party tonight. You know how forgetful your uncle can be."

Nick was immediately alarmed. Had his uncle said anything about the remains?

He felt guilty as he gazed at his mother. Maybe he

should tell her himself what he was working on. If his father's remains had been recovered—were even now awaiting identification in Erin's lab—did he have a right to keep that from her? Or should he protect her until he knew for certain his father had finally been found after eight long years of waiting?

How would she react to the news? Would she be saddened? Relieved? Did she still feel anything for Sean Gallagher?

It was strange, but even though his parents had fought bitterly at times, Nick had never doubted their love for each other. But was it possible that he was wrong about his father's murder? Could Sean Gallagher have simply gotten tired of the fighting and decided to walk out on his family?

Nick knew John had always suspected that was what had happened, but his brother hadn't known their father the way Nick had. Deep down, Nick knew there was no way Sean would have walked out on them. Because if he had, if he had valued them so little, then how could Nick ever trust anything he believed in again?

His mother was saying something else, and with an effort, Nick snapped his attention back to her. She was looking different these days, he noticed. Younger. Thinner. Prettier. She was doing something new with her hair.

"You got a new haircut," he said.

"That was months ago." She patted her hair again, almost anxiously. "I just had it trimmed today. Do you like it?"

"It's nice," he said noncommittally, but he'd liked the old style just fine. Why did she feel the need to change herself, all of a sudden? Nick thought about what Erin had told him, that his mother had gone to a party at Hillsboro with Ed Dawson. Was that the reason for the makeover?

Nick frowned. "Do you have a minute? There's something I'd like to talk to you about."

Was it his imagination, or did she suddenly look a little uneasy? She sat down across from his desk. "What's on your mind, Nick?"

He wasn't sure how to bring it up without appearing to pry into her personal life, but then, that's exactly what he was doing, wasn't it? "I heard you went to some party at Hillsboro University with Ed Dawson the other night."

His mother looked almost floored. She also appeared just the tiniest bit guilty. "How on earth did you hear about that?"

"I have a friend who works at Hillsboro. She's a forensic anthropologist I've been consulting with on a case. She mentioned she'd met you."

"Dr. Casey?" When he nodded, his mother gave him a curious look. "What a strange coincidence that you should mention her."

"Why?"

"Because I was thinking of calling her and inviting her to your grandmother's birthday party tonight. I know it's short notice, but do you think she'd want to come?"

"I have no idea," Nick answered truthfully, taken aback by his mother's suggestion.

"I thought I might ask your cousin, Miles, to go by and pick her up."

"Why the hell would you do that?"

He'd almost growled the question, and his mother stared at him in surprise. "No need to bite my head off. And please don't swear at me. Dr. Casey just moved to Chicago a couple of months ago. I don't think she has many friends here yet. I thought she and Miles might hit it off, that's all.''

"They wouldn't hit it off," Nick said, trying to control the anger the image of Erin and his cousin stirred inside him. Miles wasn't Erin's type. He was a narc, for God's sake. He didn't hang around with people like Erin. "I don't think Dr. Casey is the type of woman who would appreciate your matchmaking.''

His mother's brows rose delicately. "I didn't realize you knew her that well.''

He heard the question in her voice, but he shrugged. "I don't.''

"Well, I wouldn't want to offend her," Maggie mused. She brightened suddenly. "I know. Why don't you bring her, since you already know her? That might make her feel more comfortable. And then if she and Miles happen to meet at the party, so much the better.''

Had he walked into that one or what? Nick thought with grudging admiration. His mother had always had a way of getting what she wanted, and not only that, she'd completely steered him away from the subject he'd wanted to talk to her about in the first place.

She rose abruptly. "I'm glad that's settled. One less thing I have to worry about. Fiona is trying to keep Gran busy and out of my hair today, but you know how she gets on her birthday. The woman is just like a child. Always snooping around, looking for her presents—''

"Not so fast," Nick said as his mother headed for the door. She paused and glanced back. He came around the desk to face her. "Is Ed Dawson going to be there tonight?''

His mother blushed prettily. Not a good sign, Nick decided.

"I've invited him," she admitted.

"As your date?"

She lifted her chin almost defiantly, gazing straight into Nick's eyes. "Would that bother you?"

He wished he could tell her no, but since he couldn't, he said nothing.

Maggie sighed. "I've been alone a long time, Nick."

He felt another stab of guilt. "I know."

"In spite of the fights, I loved your father very much."

"I know that, too."

"But eight years is a long time." She reached up and stroked his cheek. "I know how hard your father's disappearance has been on you."

"We've all had a rough time," Nick said.

"Yes, that's true. But you're the one I've always worried about the most."

That surprised Nick. He gazed down at her. "Not Tony?"

"Tony's caused me untold gray hairs," she admitted ruefully. "But I always knew the right woman would someday come along and straighten him out, and Eve has. She's been wonderful for him. And John has always been, well, John. You know how he is."

"Yeah, I know how John is," Nick said, trying to keep the bitterness from his voice. The fact was, he and his older brother had never gotten along, and Nick didn't think they ever would. Since their father's disappearance, the situation between them had only gotten worse.

"Your brother is a good man, Nick. Deep down, you know that." When Nick didn't say anything, tears filled his mother's eyes. "You've never forgiven him for suggesting that your father might have walked out on us, have you?"

"Have you?" Nick demanded angrily.

"So quick to temper." She shook her head. "You've always been blinded by your emotions, Nick. That's why I worry about you."

"You don't need to worry about me."

"But I do. I want you to be happy. I want you to learn how to forgive and forget."

"Are we talking about John again?" he said with a frown.

She stared at him for a moment, looking for all the world as if she had something she wanted to tell him. Then changing her mind, she glanced away, as if no longer able to meet his gaze. "I'd better be going."

As Nick watched her leave his office, something that might have been a premonition stole over him. What had his mother been on the verge of telling him? And why hadn't she been able to look him in the eye?

ERIN'S MORNING was so hectic, she didn't have time to work in the lab, let alone spend much time thinking about Nick—although she did catch herself daydreaming about his kiss during her eight o'clock lecture. Such woolgathering was unusual for her, and she saw her students gazing at her curiously, no doubt wondering what had gotten into the staid Dr. Casey.

They would probably be surprised to learn that a passionate kiss from an attractive man had sent her into such a tailspin. Most of them were undoubtedly far more experienced than she, and by this stage of the attraction, would have been contemplating far more erotic images than kisses.

The truth of the matter was, Erin had been contemplating a few of those fantasies herself. At the most inopportune moments, she would picture herself with Nick, in bed, between satin sheets, the two of them way beyond kissing. She wasn't a virgin. She knew where those kisses would eventually lead, if she and Nick let them, and so she had no trouble at all playing out her fantasies.

"You have the look of a woman who's just gotten laid," Lois had told her bluntly when the two of them had literally run into each other in the hallway. Erin, who hadn't seen Lois coming out of a classroom, had plowed right into her.

Blushing, Erin had stammered. "Sorry. I wasn't looking where I was going."

"Obviously, but don't worry," Lois said. "All will be forgiven if you tell me what you've been up to. You were with that yummy detective last night, weren't you? The one I saw in your office the other day."

"We did have dinner together," Erin admitted. "But—"

Lois put up a hand. "That glow in your eyes says it all. Just tell me one thing." She leaned in closer. "Were there handcuffs involved?"

Between classes and paperwork, it was midafternoon before Erin finally made it down to the lab. Ross Calvert, her research assistant, came rushing over to her the moment she walked in the door. His face, usually so calm, was animated with excitement.

"We got her, Dr. Casey! The delivery from Freemont came while you were out." He pointed across the lab, where an ornate coffin had been placed in one corner.

"Ah, so we did," Erin said, her own excitement mounting.

The coffin had been unearthed in the nearby town of Freemont, Illinois, by a bulldozer operator clearing property for a new subdivision. There were no records of a cemetery ever having been at the location, and no other coffins had been dug up. The construction company, anxious to avoid bad publicity à la *Poltergeist,* was avidly trying to learn the identity of the deceased, so that she could join her relatives in some nearby cemetery.

The casket had been dated by a local historian as late nineteenth century, and he'd told Erin on the phone that the viewing window in the coffin revealed remnants of what looked to be an elaborate headdress of white lace and silk—a bridal veil—on the skull. Erin's instructions to him had been to leave the coffin sealed and ship it intact to the FAHIL lab, where a painstaking study of both the casket and the remains would hopefully provide clues to the woman's identity.

"When do you think we can open the casket?" Ross asked with almost morbid enthusiasm.

"Not for a few days," Erin said. "We have other work to finish first." As intriguing as she was, a hundred-year-old bride had to wait her turn behind the more pressing forensic cases Erin was currently working on. Especially Case 00-04.

The door to the lab opened, and Gloria stuck her head in. "Dr. Casey," she called, refusing to set foot inside the lab. When Erin started toward her, Gloria glanced over her shoulder, then lowered her voice. "You have a visitor. I hope it's okay that I brought him down."

Judging by the way Gloria was acting, Erin suspected her visitor was Nick. "Show him in."

Her pulse began to race at the thought of seeing Nick—at the memory of last night—but when Ed Dawson stepped inside the lab, an unpleasant shiver of apprehension replaced Erin's anticipation.

"Dr. Casey, good to see you again." His voice was pleasant enough, but his eyes were just as Erin remembered them—cold and expressionless.

"What can I do for you, Superintendent Dawson?" she asked politely. He was elegantly dressed in an expensive suit, his silver hair neatly combed back. The scent of his cologne mingled subtly with the disinfectants they used in the lab. Erin preferred the scent of the latter.

"I was hoping for a tour of your lab," he said as he glanced around. If the skeletal remains displayed about the lab bothered him, he certainly didn't let on. "I didn't realize your facilities were so large."

"Yes, we're fortunate to have both adequate space and the latest equipment," she said. "I'm very grateful to Hillsboro."

"Dean Stanton mentioned that an anonymous donor was responsible for all this." He glanced at Erin curiously. "You have no idea who your benefactor is?"

"No," Erin said truthfully. She hadn't given the matter much thought. "FAHIL was built before I came to Hillsboro, so the donation had nothing to do with me."

"I see." He glanced over at her worktable, where the remains of Case 00-03 had been covered. "That's one of your current cases, I presume. Perhaps you could show me a little of what you do here."

Erin hesitated, then shrugged. "Let me call over my

research assistant. He and I have been working together on this case.''

After Erin had made the introductions, she said, ''Ross, perhaps you would like to explain our findings to Superintendent Dawson.''

Ross's brows lifted slightly as he gazed from Erin to Dawson. ''Cool.''

He pulled on a pair of gloves, then peeled back the covering from the remains, revealing the pristine skeleton. ''She was found beneath an old house that was being torn down in Chinatown,'' he said. Then carefully, Ross narrated their findings, explaining how they'd determined the woman's age, race, height, weight, and cause and manner of death.

''We just found out her name is Nancy Wong,'' he told Dawson. ''Detective Stoner thinks her husband killed her nearly ten years ago, then fled the country. Dr. Casey was able to pinpoint her from a list of missing persons fitting her general physical description and time of disappearance because she was the only one who was a marathon runner.''

Dawson looked slightly taken aback. ''You could tell that by looking at her bones?''

''Pretty cool, huh?'' Ross grinned at Erin.

''I'm intrigued,'' Dawson said. ''How on earth were you able to tell the woman was a runner, Dr. Casey?''

''I didn't know for sure. It was an educated guess.'' Erin showed him the muscle attachment markings on the leg bones and knee joints, explaining that the grainy ridges indicated the woman's legs had been heavily muscled.

''You'd be surprised what Dr. Casey can read from bones,'' Ross told Dawson proudly. ''She's a genius. We're lucky to have her at FAHIL.''

"I've heard phenomenal things about you," Dawson said slowly, his gaze cool and appraising on Erin. "I'm beginning to believe they may not have been exaggerated."

NICK WAS STILL thinking about his mother when he pulled into the parking lot near FAHIL. He was certain she'd had something on her mind, something she'd wanted to tell him, but for whatever reason, she hadn't been able to confide in him. What was she hiding? The seriousness of her relationship with Ed Dawson? Or something else? Something about his father, maybe? Had she found out about the remains?

Nick knew he wouldn't be able to keep the discovery a secret much longer. The small newspaper in Webber County had carried a full account that morning of Clive Avery's murder and the excavation of the skeleton. And though neither Nick nor Erin had been mentioned by name, it wouldn't take much digging by a nosy reporter to figure out that Sean Gallagher had disappeared under suspicious circumstances from that area eight years ago. Given the recent publicity concerning Daniel O'Roarke's imminent release from prison, Nick figured it was only a matter of time before the Chicago papers ran with the story. He couldn't delay much longer in telling his family.

He parked in the faculty parking area near FAHIL, using his police department tag to keep from getting towed. As he got out of his car, he automatically glanced around, his gaze resting on a black Mercedes sedan that had pulled to the curb in a no-parking zone. The windows were so heavily tinted that he could barely make out the silhouette of the driver, who seemed to be waiting for someone inside the building.

But as Nick continued to stare at the vehicle, the car pulled away from the curb and nosed its way through the parking lot. As it passed by Nick's car, the driver turned and stared at him for a moment before accelerating out of the parking lot in a manner that seemed almost defiant.

Nick jotted down the license plate number in his notebook, then reached for his phone. Within seconds, the number had been entered into the system.

IT WAS TWILIGHT by the time Nick left Erin's office. He'd been too late to warn her about a possible call from his mother because Maggie had been too quick. She'd already phoned Erin, and to Nick's surprise, Erin had accepted the invitation to his grandmother's birthday party. She'd even seemed please by the invitation, and more than a little curious about the rest of his family.

Nick didn't know what Erin would think of his family once she met them. He was pretty sure they weren't what she was expecting. She had some idealistic view of what families were supposed to be like, but the Gallaghers didn't fit any mold that Nick was aware of. They closed ranks when threatened by some outside force, like the O'Roarkes, but within, tempers, resentment, even petty jealousy at times, ran rampant.

As he walked across the parking lot toward his car, he had the unmistakable sensation of being watched. Reaching inside his jacket, he unsnapped his shoulder holster, but didn't remove his gun as he casually scanned his surroundings.

At this hour, the campus was sparsely populated, with only an occasional student or faculty member hurrying along the shaded walkways, barely glancing in

Nick's direction. He thought at first he'd imagined the feeling, but then his gaze lit on a tall man standing in the shadow of the FAHIL building. As Nick continued to watch, the man took a step toward him, staring back, then suddenly he spun on his heel and disappeared around the building, in the direction of the alley.

Nick followed him, glancing over his shoulder periodically to make sure he wasn't being set up for an ambush. As he entered the alley, dusk became darkness, and the security lights afforded only patches of illumination. The man was standing at the back of the alley, near the wall that created a dead end. Apprehension settled over Nick as he approached the man cautiously. There was something familiar about him, something a little disturbing.

"You're not being followed," the man said from the shadows, as if sensing Nick's unease.

At the sound of the man's voice, Nick relaxed slightly. He knew that voice, though he'd never met the man face-to-face before. The informant known as Fisher had always called when he had information for Nick, or arranged to meet in remote locations in the dead of night. He'd always taken precautions to keep his identity hidden, but that wasn't unusual. Informants walked a very thin line, balancing precariously between the law and the criminals they sold out.

Unlike other informants, Fisher had never asked Nick for money. He'd never asked for anything, which made Nick more than a little suspicious. What did Fisher really want from him? A connection to the police? Self-importance? Not unusual, either, in an informant.

When Nick moved toward him, Fisher drew back into the shadows. "That's far enough."

"What do you want?" Nick asked with a frown. How the hell had Fisher known where to find him— unless he'd been following him?

"You've been asking around about Clive Avery." The voice, purposefully distorted, drove Nick's uneasiness even deeper.

He nodded. "How did you know that?"

"I got sources."

It was those sources that worried Nick. "You know something about Avery?"

"He used to be CPD."

"Tell me something I don't know."

Fisher paused. "He was in the Detective Division eight years ago."

That stopped Nick cold. Eight years ago, his father had been in the Detective Division. Was there a connection? "Who did he work with?"

Fisher shrugged. "He worked south side mainly. He had a partner named Donnelly, but I don't think he's still on the force. Last I heard, he moved to Indiana."

"Why was Avery dismissed?"

"He left before there was a formal review, but word on the street was that he was on the take."

A dirty cop. Nick had suspected as much. "Who was he working for? The O'Roarkes?"

"That I can't tell you. But if I were you, I'd talk to some of the guys who were in the Detective Division back then. Find out what they remember about Avery. Who he was close to. Who he might have talked to. Who he might have still been in touch with. There's where you're going to find your lead."

"Did you know Avery?" Nick wasn't sure where the question came from, but he knew all of a sudden that Fisher had once been a cop. "Were you in the

Detective Division eight years ago?'' When Fisher didn't answer, Nick said almost angrily, ''Did you know my father?''

''Don't ask questions you don't want the answers to,'' Fisher said gruffly.

Chapter Ten

"Clive Avery may have been the leak after all," Nick told Erin that night, as they drove south, toward his old neighborhood.

"You've learned something new?"

Nick shrugged, thinking about Fisher's tip. "I've got a lead or two I'm working on. Plus, we're checking through Avery's e-mail. He had quite a few cyber buddies he corresponded with regularly."

"And you think one of them might have killed him?"

"We don't know that," Nick said. "But the point is, he liked to talk. The sheriff's department is trying to trace some of the correspondence, but Webber County is not exactly up on the latest technology."

"So, they still don't have any real clues."

Nick hesitated. Actually, the e-mail was a fairly significant clue as far as he was concerned, because Daniel O'Roarke had access to a computer in prison. What bothered Nick now was Fisher's last cryptic remark. *Don't ask questions you don't want answers to.* What the hell had he meant by that? And who was Fisher, anyway? Why had he sought out Nick when there were dozens of detectives he could have made contact with?

Erin shifted in her seat, leaning toward him slightly, and he caught a whiff of her perfume, that deep, sensual fragrance that had seemed contradictory at first— but that was before he'd kissed her. Now her scent seemed a perfect match. Deep, sensual and more than a little intriguing.

Nick could hardly keep his eyes off her tonight. She wore a simple dark-blue dress that complemented her eyes and made her slight body look both elegant and curvy—almost too inviting. But it was her hair that had captured Nick's attention the moment he'd first laid eyes on her.

She'd left it down to cascade in gleaming curls over her shoulders and down her back, and Nick wanted nothing more than to touch it, to hold fistfuls of it to his nose and drink in the fragrance he knew would be intoxicating.

Her hair was every man's fantasy.

He wanted her, he realized suddenly. Now. Forget his grandmother's birthday party. Maybe he and Erin should just go back to his place—

"Nick?"

He could tell from her tone that she'd asked a question a second time and he still hadn't responded. He scowled briefly at the road. "Sorry. Drifted off there for a moment. What were you saying?"

"I asked about your family. Tell me about them."

"I wouldn't know where to start."

"How about your brothers?" she prompted. "They're on the police force as well, right?"

"Yeah. John's the oldest. He just made lieutenant a few months ago, and he also recently got married. His wife's name is Thea, and she has a little girl named Nikki. My younger brother is Tony, and he's currently

involved with a woman named Eve Barrett. She's also
a cop, Internal Affairs, which, with Tony's history,
makes for an interesting pair," he said dryly.

"What do you mean?"

"Tony is—" Nick lifted his hand to rub the back of
his neck. "Let's just say my little brother likes to walk
on the wild side, and Eve's pretty straight. I had my
doubts about their relationship at first, but she's turned
out to be the best thing that ever happened to him."

"What about your brother John?"

"What about him?"

"Are you and he close?"

"Not especially."

Erin sighed. "That's too bad." Her voice sounded
oddly wistful. "I've always wanted a brother."

Nick glanced at her curiously. "You don't have any
brothers or sisters?"

She hesitated, turning to stare out the window for a
moment. "I don't have anyone since my mother died.
You don't know how lucky you are, coming from a
big family. You should cherish them, Nick. You don't
know what it's like to be so completely alone."

He felt a pang of guilt at her words, and he thought,
not for the first time, that he might wake up one day
and find that it was too late to make amends with John.
They were both cops. Anything could happen in the
line of duty. Would his grudge offer him any comfort
then?

"You're probably right," he said. "I've been thinking about my sister a lot lately. I'm worried about her."

"Is she sick?" Erin asked with instant concern.

It was Nick's turn to hesitate. He scowled at the
road, not exactly comfortable with airing his family's
dirty laundry. "She was in love with this man. She'd

known him for a long time. We all knew him. He and Tony were best friends. Or at least, that's what we all thought. But then he killed three women and tried to frame Tony for the murders. He almost killed Fiona. Since then…'' He trailed off, not certain how much more he should tell Erin. Obviously, she had a fairy-tale notion of what families should be like, but the Gallaghers weren't exactly the Brady Bunch.

Aside from the decades-old feud with the O'Roarkes, there were internal problems and clashes, as well. A family of cops hardly made for serene family gatherings. The get-togethers were as likely as not to be noisy, bawdy and sometimes downright unbearable. His grandmother's birthday party would probably be no exception.

Nick wondered if Erin's opinion of family—and of him—might change after spending an evening with the Gallaghers.

THEY WERE WONDERFUL! All of them. Exactly the way Erin had always imagined a big family would be.

She gazed around the crowded living room, her eyes and ears feasting on the noisy revel of the Gallaghers. She felt a little like Sandra Bullock in *While You Were Sleeping*. Not only was she falling in a big way for Nick Gallagher, but she was instantly in love with his whole family.

Nick's grandmother, who, with her lovely complexion and vibrant red hair looked very much like Maureen O'Hara, was energetically dancing an Irish jig with her son Liam, while the whole crowd laughed and clapped in time to the tune. Erin, who had never had any particular rhythm, felt her own toes tapping as if of their own volition. It was that kind of music and that kind of evening.

Although she hadn't formally met everyone yet, she could pick out faces in the crowd from Nick's earlier descriptions. Nick's older brother, John, twirled an adorable little girl in a yellow party dress in time to the music while his beautiful wife, Thea, watched them indulgently.

Tony, looking dark and faintly sinister in his leather jacket, draped a casual arm across the shoulders of a woman dressed primly in a business suit, stockings and heels. At first glance, the pair appeared mismatched, as Nick had said, but then Erin saw the way the two of them looked at each other, the whispers they shared, and she couldn't help envying them. What would it be like to have a man look at her that way? To have someone care about her the way Tony so obviously cared about Eve? The way John so obviously worshipped Thea and her daughter?

The Gallaghers were so lucky, Erin thought sadly. And they didn't even know it.

Across the room, another couple stood apart from the crowd, as if they didn't quite belong to the celebration. The woman had the characteristic Gallagher dark hair and blue eyes, but it was the man who drew Erin's attention, simply because he'd been staring at her off and on all evening.

A vague recognition tugged at Erin. There was something about him...

"You must be Erin," a soft voice said at her side.

Erin knew at once who the stunning redhead was. Fiona Gallagher had the kind of striking beauty that caused heads to turn when she walked into the room, but the smattering of freckles across her nose gave her a kind of unaffected charm that made her seem approachable. Her blue eyes were shadowed with pain, and Erin remembered what Nick had told her about his sister. She'd been deeply hurt by a man she was in love with, and Erin felt a certain kinship with the young woman. She was no stranger to pain, either.

"And you're Nick's sister," she said, extending her hand.

"How did you know?" the redhead asked warily.

"You look exactly like your grandmother."

"If only I had her common sense," Fiona muttered.

"I beg your pardon?"

Fiona shrugged, but her gaze on Erin was oddly intense. "So tell me, how did you and Nick meet?"

"I'm consulting with him on a case."

"You're a forensics anthropologist, right? Mother was very impressed with you when she met you."

Erin's brows lifted. "Really? I'm flattered. I liked her, too."

Fiona smiled a little. "Mother can be a real sweetheart. I mean that. I know it's not all that PC to be close to your parents these days, but if it hadn't been for her—" She broke off, and shrugged. "Never mind. You don't need to hear all about my sordid past. Tell me about the case you and Nick are consulting on."

Erin hesitated. "I don't really like to talk about my work. A lot of what I do is confidential."

Fiona nodded, not the least offended. "I understand. Believe me, there are things I don't like to talk about, either."

Erin thought again of the man who had broken Fiona's heart. A man who had murdered three women, and tried to blame Nick's brother. The Gallaghers, for all their closeness, were a very complicated family.

As if reading her mind, Fiona said softly, "So, tell me about you and Nick."

Erin's heart started to beat in slow, painful ticks. "There's nothing to tell. Nick and I are just—"

"Friends. I know. That's what Thea told me about her and John."

"No, really. Nick and I are working together on a case," Erin explained, not wanting Fiona to misconstrue their relationship. What better way to chase Nick away than to have his family make premature assumptions?

"And that's what Eve said about her and Tony. You may as well hang it up, Erin, and face facts. Nick wouldn't have brought you here if he didn't have plans for you. He just doesn't know it, yet. My brothers can all be pretty dense, but then, I'm not exactly in a position to criticize," she added ironically.

Erin had been enjoying herself before, but now, with Fiona, she felt completely out of her element. She wasn't used to Fiona's bluntness, and Erin wondered if such frankness came with having a large family. Did no one keep secrets?

Erin wasn't so sure she could handle that. She'd lived with the secret of her own family for so long, it was a part of her. She'd grown up knowing there were things she didn't talk about, parts of her life she always had to keep hidden.

Fiona smiled. "I didn't mean to make you uncomfortable. I'm sorry. It's just that I know my brother so well. He can be like a dog with a bone when it comes to his work, but his personal life is another matter. He might need a little push in the right direction from time to time."

Was that why his mother had invited her here? Erin

wondered. Was Maggie Gallagher giving Nick that push?

But if they weren't careful, they might push him completely away. Nick wasn't the type of man who would appreciate being manipulated. He had his own mind, and he wouldn't like someone trying to change it.

She spotted him across the room just then, and their gazes met. He was looking at her the way he'd looked at her that first night on Dean Stanton's portico, as if he wasn't quite certain she was the woman he thought she was.

Then, very slowly, he started toward her, and Erin's heart began to race. He wore black jeans and a black pullover sweater, and for some reason, his eyes looked even bluer tonight. A vivid, compelling blue that sent shivers up and down Erin's spine.

For a moment, as she watched Nick move toward her through the crowd, Erin forgot all about his sister standing beside her. Then Fiona said softly, "Just friends, huh? I don't think so...."

NICK DECIDED it was time to get Erin alone for a few minutes. For one thing, he didn't trust what Fiona might be telling her, and for another, he didn't much like the way his cousin Miles kept staring at her. If Nick wasn't careful, he just might decide he had to do something about it.

But before he could reach Erin's side, his uncle stopped him. "I need to have a word with you, Nick."

Nick started to protest, but then shrugged, flashing Erin an apologetic look before following his uncle into the kitchen.

"So, what have you found out?" Liam demanded.

"Nothing conclusive." Nick leaned against the counter, glancing around the freshly painted kitchen. His mother had spruced the room up with new curtains and bright throw rugs, but it still looked pretty much the same as Nick remembered it growing up, when the family had gathered around the large, pine table for hasty meals before school and ball games.

He turned back to his uncle. "The remains are still being examined, but it appears he may have been strangled."

"Strangled?" Liam looked shocked. "I wasn't expecting that."

"Neither was I."

"Damn it," his uncle said grimly. "That means no murder weapon. No evidence."

Nick had thought of that, but he wasn't about to give up. "Not necessarily. I still think Daniel O'Roarke is the type of guy who would talk. He was always full of himself. He couldn't keep something like this to himself. He'd have to brag about it."

"You have a lead?" Liam asked anxiously.

"Maybe," Nick evaded. "He has access to a computer in prison. I'd like to know who he's been corresponding with."

"I don't get this, Nick. Sean was a big man. He kept himself in shape. How the hell did that son of a bitch O'Roarke manage to strangle him?"

Nick shrugged. "Daniel's a big man himself. Plus, he was a lot younger than Dad, and he had the element of surprise. I think he followed Dad to the cabin, caught him off guard, hit him in the back of the head, then strangled him. The knife was what tripped him up in Ashley's murder. He didn't make that mistake a second time. Without a murder weapon or a body, he got away with it.''

''You can prove Sean was murdered?'' Liam pressed.

''Not yet,'' Nick admitted. He turned, glancing out the kitchen window, watching shadows move in the backyard. He remembered the smoke he'd smelled last night. The barking dog. The overwhelming sense that his father had been near. Was that a sign he was getting close to the truth? ''Someone went to a lot of trouble to make sure the remains couldn't be easily identified. That smells like murder to me.''

Liam's mouth hardened in hatred. ''Yeah, but proving it is a whole different matter. The O'Roarkes know what they're doing, Nick. The bastards know how to cover their tracks.''

''But they're not invincible. They made a big mistake when they killed Clive Avery.''

''What do you mean?''

''He could be the link to the O'Roarkes I've been looking for. I'm thinking he's the one who tipped Daniel O'Roarke about the discovery of the remains and the excavation. Whether it was inadvertent or intentional, I don't know. But Avery used to be a CPD cop. He was in the Detective Division. Did you know him?''

''Can't say as I remember the name.''

''I think he may have been on the O'Roarkes' payroll. He got dismissed from CPD, so they put him in Webber County, where they knew someday they might need him.''

''The O'Roarkes are powerful,'' Liam said darkly, ''but, hell, even they can't see the future. How could they know Sean's body would someday be discovered?''

"They didn't. But like you said, they know how to cover their tracks.''

Liam put a hand on Nick's shoulder. "Be careful,'' he said gruffly. "I don't want to lose you to the O'Roarkes like we lost Sean. Or like I lost Katie.''

Nick wanted to remind Liam that his daughter was still very much alive, but his uncle wasn't the type to forgive or forget, not even his own flesh and blood. Liam's attitude struck a little too close to home, and Nick shifted uncomfortably, aware of his own inflexible stance.

Ironically, the first person he saw when he left the kitchen was Dylan O'Roarke, standing with his wife, Kaitlin. Dylan and Kaitlin had been barred from ever setting foot in Liam's house, but Nick's mother had made it clear to them from the first that they would always be welcome in her home. Nick had always made a point of avoiding Dylan at family gatherings, which meant that he also had to avoid Kaitlin, even though the two of them had been close as children. He felt a prickle of regret now as he watched her.

Across the room, his cousin caught him staring at her, and she smiled tentatively. Nick returned her smile. Kaitlin looked almost shocked, but then her smile slowly widened in pleasure.

Beside her, Dylan O'Roarke gazed at Nick with the same wariness Nick couldn't help feeling toward him. Toward any O'Roarke. Like his uncle, Nick's bitterness had been too deeply ingrained for too many years. He didn't trust any of the O'Roarkes, and he didn't think he ever would.

NICK SAID in Erin's ear, "So, what do you think? Are you ready to run screaming from here in terror?"

Erin, her pulse racing at Nick's nearness, said earnestly, "Your family is wonderful. This is just the way I imagined it would be."

His smiled seemed almost tender as he gazed down at her. "You're looking at us through rose-colored glasses. Wait till you get to know us better."

Erin's heart skipped a bit. Get to know them better? Did he mean...was he implying...? She drew a long, steadying breath. "I look forward to that," she tried to say calmly.

"So do I." His gaze on her was so intense, Erin felt everything inside her still. The party noises faded along with her doubts. She could see the desire swirling in Nick's eyes, and the knowledge that he wanted her bolstered her confidence and courage in a way she would never have believed possible. She touched a hand to his chest, a small gesture really, but one that seemed to bond them unexpectedly.

He took her hand, and she thought at first he meant to lift it to his lips, but instead, he pulled her to a small, darkened alcove beneath the stairs.

"Erin, listen." He gazed down at her, his eyes so dark a blue they almost seemed black. "I don't know what's going on here, what this is between you and me...." He trailed off, as if unsure of himself suddenly. Which thrilled Erin. That a man like Nick could be feeling as off balance as she...

"You know I like you. I admire and respect you. God knows I'm attracted to you...."

Don't stop now, Erin thought with a delicious shiver. "I feel the same way about you," she offered shyly.

"I know we haven't known each other very long."

Long enough, she wanted to tell him. "No, we haven't."

"I don't mean to rush you, but I just thought you should know that I—" He reached up to touch her hair, and his eyes closed briefly. "Damn," he whispered.

Erin took a step toward him, placing both hands on his chest. Without another word, Nick buried his hands in her hair, wrapping his fingers around the long, curly strands as his head lowered toward hers.

He teased her at first, letting the tip of his tongue outline her lips before slipping inside to tangle with hers. Erin swayed against him, the wine, the night, everything making her feel heady and bold. She wound her arms around him as he literally swept her off her feet, lifting her easily and holding her against him until their hearts were beating against one another.

Erin didn't want to resist him, and so she didn't. She let herself go, throwing all her emotions, all her secret yearnings into that one kiss. Her hand slipped along his jawline, gently caressing, before her fingers slid to the back of his neck, entangling themselves in his hair.

And Nick responded at once. Oh, did he respond! He carried her deeper into the corner, letting her body slide wantonly down his as he pressed her against the wall, his broad shoulders shielding her from prying eyes. His hands and mouth were like magic, white-hot enchantment that bewitched her with desire, mesmerized her with plain, old-fashioned lust.

But it was more than that. She wanted to know every part of him intimately—his mind and soul as well as his body. And she wanted him to know her.

That thought almost stopped her. Did she really want Nick to know the real *her?* The family she'd been born into? The name she'd once had?

Would he understand why she kept that part of her life a secret, or would he, being a cop, paint her with the sins of her father?

The strands of "Happy Birthday" finally brought them both back to their senses, and Nick reluctantly released Erin. She said shakily, "They're singing 'Happy Birthday' to your grandmother. You should be out there."

"Okay." But he made no move to leave. His gaze was dark and longing, a little frightening, Erin decided, because she'd never known a man so intense.

"We won't stay much longer," he promised. "After Gran opens her presents, we can leave."

Erin shivered in anticipation as they went back out to join the party. Would they say good-night at her door tonight, or did she dare invite Nick inside?

"I'VE BEEN WONDERING when I'd get to meet you," Colleen Gallagher said in a lilting Irish brogue. Her gaze swept Erin from head to toe. "Why, Nick, she's just a tiny little thing. You'd make two of her."

"She's not so small," Nick said with a grin. Not where it counts, his eyes seemed to tell Erin. "She can hold her own, Gran, trust me."

"Oh, I don't doubt that," his grandmother said thoughtfully, studying Erin with a shrewdness that might have been unnerving if not for the twinkle in her blue, blue eyes.

"Happy birthday, Mrs. Gallagher," Erin said politely.

"Call me Colleen. Mrs. Gallagher makes me seem so old."

Erin had no idea the woman's age, but she had grown grandchildren, so she had to be at least in her eighties. But her eyes were a brilliant, flashing blue, and her hair an impossible red. Unlike Fiona, Erin suspected Colleen used an enhancement, but the result suited her to a T. The vibrant woman would have looked positively unnatural with gray hair.

She waved a hand at her grandson. "Run along, Nick. Give Erin and me a chance to get acquainted."

Nick frowned. "We were just leaving, Gran."

Colleen arched a stern brow. "Surely you can spare a few minutes for your poor old grandmother."

He gave Erin a dry look. "Now she's old, all of a sudden, because she wants to get her way. Okay," he said to Colleen affectionately, bending to kiss her cheek. "She's all yours. But I'm coming back in ten minutes."

"Ah, to be so young and energetic again," Colleen said wistfully, gazing after her grandson. She shook off the melancholy and took Erin's hand. "Let's sit down for a while."

Once they were settled on the sofa, Colleen turned, scanning Erin's face curiously. "You look very familiar to me. Have we met before?"

"I don't think so," Erin said. "I'm new to Chicago."

Colleen put her hand beneath Erin's chin, turning her face one way and then the other. After a moment, she said almost gently, "You're Irish, aren't you?"

Erin stared at her in shock. She hadn't been called by that name since she was a baby. Since the day she and her mother had left town. "How did you know—?"

Colleen smiled. "That complexion," she said. "Who else has skin like that except for the Irish?"

Erin's breath caught in her throat. How could she

have misunderstood Colleen's meaning? She never had before. In all these years, Erin had never once given away her secret identity. She never thought of herself as Irish, even though that was the name she'd been given at birth. But her mother had legally changed both their names after leaving Chicago, and Erin had become Erin Casey in every way that counted.

Colleen was still studying her. "You know, I believe I've figured out why you look so familiar to me. You remind me of someone I knew a long time ago."

A tingle of apprehension stole over Erin, though she wasn't sure why. "Who was it?"

Colleen smiled sadly. "A man I was once very much in love with. His name was James O'Roarke."

Chapter Eleven

Erin was so quiet on the way home, Nick started to worry about her. Had she disliked his family that much? Was she ready to wash her hands of the lot of them?

As if sensing his gaze on her, she turned and their eyes met for only a split second before she glanced away.

Nick pulled to the curb in front of her apartment and shut off the engine. For the longest moment, they sat without speaking. Then, almost cautiously, he draped his arm over the back of her seat, letting his fingers sweep against her hair.

"Erin, what's wrong?"

She glanced at him finally, her eyes shadowed in the streetlight. She made a helpless gesture with her hand. "I'm just tired, I guess."

She wasn't just tired. She was a completely different woman from the one he'd kissed earlier. That Erin had been passionate and impulsive, a seductress who had made him almost crazy from wanting her. This Erin was cool and remote. Untouchable.

He said almost grimly, "Did I miss something back there?"

She shot him a wary glance. "What do you mean?"

"I mean, did I read you wrong?"

She drew a long, shaky breath. "You didn't read me wrong. It's just…"

"What?"

She shrugged. "Things are moving a little too fast for me. It's like you said. We haven't known each other that long."

"Okay." He leaned toward her, letting his hand skim through her hair, then cupping the back of her neck. "But we can fix that, can't we? Will you go out with me tomorrow night?"

She looked taken aback by his question. "You mean on a date?"

He smiled. "Why not? Cops are allowed to date."

"But the case…isn't there some rule—"

"Not that I'm aware of. How about if I pick you up here, we go out to dinner or to a movie, maybe talk a little afterward and get to know each other."

"And…then?" Her eyes were a soft misty blue in the streetlight.

"Then we do it again, or at least variations of it, until we…I don't know…trust each other. Until we're both ready to take another step. Does that sound about right to you?"

"I haven't dated in a long time," she said almost apologetically.

He wound a strand of her hair around his finger. "It's like riding a bike. You never forget how. After what we've been through, dating should be a piece of cake."

"You may not like me once you get to know me," Erin warned.

"I don't think that's possible." Her face looked pale

in the streetlight. Pale and a little strained. Nick wasn't convinced the brevity of their relationship was her real concern here.

They got out of the car and he walked her to her door. At the top of the stairs, he said, "Could we sit out here for a while? It's a nice night and I don't think I'm ready to go home."

Erin knew what he meant. She faced the same emptiness inside her own apartment. The same loneliness. She wasn't eager to end the night, either, although she knew it would be best for them both if she did. After her talk with Nick's grandmother's, Erin's past had come back to haunt her, casting a pall over the whole evening.

She'd been Erin Casey almost all her life, but suddenly, because of a chance remark by Nick's grandmother, the ghost of Irish O'Roarke was suddenly hovering over her, making her doubt herself in a way she hadn't in a very long time.

Erin had been a devoted daughter, a gifted student, and now a respected forensic anthropologist. She knew that she was a successful person, a decent person who'd worked very hard to make her life worthwhile. But even after all these years, even with no memory of what he looked like, her father's presence, his influence, still lurked in the deepest recesses of her mind.

She wondered now what Nick would think of her if she suddenly blurted out the truth. *I'm James O'Roarke's granddaughter. The man your grandmother used to be in love with. The man who built a crime empire that has defied the law for years.*

The irony was almost overwhelming. That she and Nick were connected in ways they'd never even known about—

They sat down on the top step, their shoulders brushing, and for a while they remained silent. The night was cool, but they both had on jackets, and the wind was more invigorating than sharp. The glow of city lights obliterated the stars, but a waxing moon hung low in the sky, milky white and romantic.

"Why have you never married, Nick?" she asked after a bit.

She sensed his surprise at the question, but he shrugged. "I guess I could give you the stock answer and say I've never met the right woman. But I've been involved in a serious relationship or two. Who knows? Maybe they could have worked out if I'd given them a chance."

"Why didn't you?"

"Cops make lousy husbands, Erin. My parents used to argue and fight constantly. Mostly about my dad's work. I know they loved each other, but I always promised myself I wouldn't put any woman through what my mother went through."

"So you've stayed alone all these years."

He shrugged again.

"Don't you ever get lonely?" She heard the wistfulness in her own voice, and when he turned to stare at her, she saw something of her own soul mirrored in his eyes.

"I'm lonely right now," he said softly.

Erin's heart beat an unsteady rhythm inside her. "Why?" she asked almost in a whisper.

His gaze on her deepened. "Because I think we had something back there, a moment when things could have worked out for us. But I'm thinking now that we may have lost it and I don't even know why." He paused, staring down at her. "Did we lose it, Erin?"

She closed her eyes briefly. "I don't know. I hope not."

"I hope not, either." She felt his hand against her face, and she opened her eyes. He wove his fingers through her hair, turning her gently until they were facing each other, until their mouths were only a breath apart. Then, very slowly, he kissed her, his lips hardly more than a whisper against hers.

Erin trembled at the touch, at his nearness, at the emotions churning inside her. And she knew, without a doubt, she was falling in love with him.

"I don't want to lose it," she whispered again, reaching up to trail a fingertip along his jawline. "I don't want to lose you."

Their eyes held for the longest moment, then Nick took her hand in his, lifting her fingers to his lips, skimming each one with a butterfly kiss that made her heart thud almost painfully. Slowly he stood and pulled her to her feet.

ERIN QUIVERED in anticipation. Nick, shirtless, sat on the edge of her bed, and she stood between his legs, facing him, staring down at him. They were both in a state of semiundress, and Erin suddenly experienced a case of nerves. Would he find her lacking? She was small, but she wasn't one of those gleaming hard bodies one saw in athletic magazines. She hated running and rarely had time for the gym. She realized now that she should have made the time. Nick's body, by comparison, was toned and magnificent.

She held her breath, the anticipation almost painful as she waited for him to say something, do something. Should she make the first move? Should she turn tail and run away as fast as she could?

Too late. Nick skimmed his hands along her bare arms, and when she shivered, his smile was knowing. His fingers moved to her back, deftly unfastening her bra, and then his hand lowered, removing the rest of her clothing. When she stood before him, encumbered only by her natural shyness, Nick said in a ragged whisper, "You take my breath away."

A cliché maybe, but Erin didn't care because his voice told her he meant it. His eyes told her he wanted her. His body, when he undressed, too, made her believe it.

She placed her hands tentatively on his shoulders, and he groaned, drawing her to him, burying his head against her breasts, caressing her, tasting her, making her shiver violently with need.

He lay back on the bed, pulling her with him, and Erin felt a secret sense of power as she rose over him. His hands were on her hips, guiding her, urging her, and the last of her shyness—and her loneliness— melted away.

SHE WAS SO beautiful and she smelled so wonderful and the things she was doing to him—

Nick opened his eyes, watching her. Her head was flung back, and her hair moved sensuously against her bare skin, inflaming his senses even more. He reached up and pulled her to him, kissing her deeply, hearing her soft, gasping breath as her hair curtained them in silk.

How had he ever thought her only attractive? She was incredible. A woman with hidden passions and deep, dark desires. A woman both shy and wanton, both needy and demanding. A perfect lover. A perfect woman. And if Nick wasn't careful, he could very easily fall in love with her.

But the timing is all wrong, remember? a voice whispered inside him.

"Shut up," Nick muttered.

Erin gazed down at him. "What?"

He buried his hands in her hair, pulling her back to him. "You're just so beautiful...." His voice trailed off as he captured her mouth once again. He rolled them, so that he was over her now, but their bodies still clung.

After a moment, her gaze widened for one split second as she stared up at him. She looked almost startled. "Nick..."

"I know," he said raggedly. "I know..."

IT WAS ALMOST DAWN. They'd spent the night making love, a little desperately the first time, more slowly the second time, and the third...

Erin shivered as she lay in the crook of Nick's arm, having only one regret. That she hadn't told him before who her father was, the kind of family she'd come from. There should have been no secrets between them for what they'd shared tonight—and she didn't mean just the sex, although that had been glorious. She wouldn't deny that.

But what had occurred between them was so much more than that. The holding, the caressing, the trust. It had taken an incredible amount of trust, at least on her part, to let herself go like that, to open herself up to the possibilities, and Nick...

She drew a long breath. Nick had been everything a woman could want in a lover. Tender. Caring. Passionate. At times even demanding, but never in a way that made Erin feel threatened. Never in a way that made her feel anything less than cherished.

And he'd trusted her, too. He'd murmured things to her in the heat of passion that Erin instinctively knew he would never have otherwise uttered. He'd shown her a glimpse of his own vulnerability, his own hidden desires, and Erin realized afterward what a rare gift he'd given her. One she wasn't sure she deserved.

"I need to tell you something," she said uncertainly.

She felt his body tense slightly. "You don't have a husband hidden away somewhere, do you?"

He was only half joking, she thought. "No. Nothing like that. I just thought you should know that I wasn't born with the name Erin Casey."

"What?"

"My mother had both our names legally changed after she and my father were divorced."

"Why?"

Erin shrugged. "She felt threatened by him. He had…criminal tendencies, to put it delicately."

"He was dangerous?" Nick's arm around her tightened protectively. Possessively. Erin thrilled to his touch.

"My mother thought so. But that's not the only reason she took me away. She didn't want me influenced by him."

"I can understand that," Nick said almost grimly. "Did your father ever try to find you?"

"Not that I know of. He and my mother had a bargain. If she gave him sole custody of my brother, she could take me as far away as she wanted to." Erin tried to swallow past the bitterness. Even after all these years, the abandonment still hurt, the bargain still rankled. Her father hadn't wanted her enough to fight for her. She should be grateful, knowing what she knew about him, but deep inside, that little girl who had longed for a family still lurked in despair. The daughter who craved her father's love and approval still haunted her.

She sighed deeply, and Nick wrapped both his arms around her, holding her close. "I can't imagine anyone ever agreeing to let you go."

Erin's heart melted. "Do you always know the right thing to say?"

"Hardly ever," he said dryly. "I'm not much of a diplomat. Just ask my brother."

"Why aren't you and he close? What happened between you two?" When Nick didn't say anything, Erin lifted her head to stare at him. "I'm sorry. I don't mean to pry. I wanted you to know about me...about my background because I thought it might—" She hesitated. "I thought it might make a difference to you."

"Why?"

She turned in his arms to study him. "My father was a criminal. Yours was a cop. *You're* a cop."

He tucked her hair behind her ear. "You aren't responsible for what your father did, Erin."

"I know that. Intellectually, I know that. But still—"

"I guess we all have doubts about ourselves." His tone sounded ironic.

"Even you?"

He grimaced. "Why does that surprise you?"

"Because you seem so self-assured, I guess. Always so in control."

"Not always." His hand trailed down her side, skimming her bare hip and making her shiver. Erin knew what he meant. He'd lost control earlier, just as she had. They'd both let go in a way she knew neither of them were used to. It was important now how they handle that intimacy. If they grew closer, or turned away from it.

After a moment, Nick said, "My father was murdered several years ago, but his body was never found. John thought there was a chance that he hadn't been killed, that he'd just up and walked out on us."

"That's why you don't get along?" Erin asked carefully.

"That's part of it. Most of it, I guess. I was closer to my father than John was. I know he would never do something like that, but sometimes—"

When he didn't finish his thought, Erin said softly, "Sometimes you've wondered about him yourself?"

"I didn't say that," Nick almost snapped.

She pulled away from him, propping herself on her elbow to gaze down at him. His face looked angry in the moonlight. Angry and hard and almost frighteningly resolved.

"You said it yourself," Erin reminded him. "We all have doubts."

"About myself, maybe. Not about him." When Erin didn't say anything, Nick glanced at her. His eyes in the dim light were dark and shadowed, almost haunted. "I can't have doubts about my own father, Erin. He was like a hero to me. I looked up to him. If he was the kind of man who could walk out on his family—" He broke off, gazing up at the ceiling. "What would that say about me?"

"You aren't responsible for your father's actions any more than I am for mine."

But Nick didn't seem to hear her. "The other night, I had the strongest sense that he was still alive, that he was…watching me, that John may have been right all these years. I know that's crazy. I know he's dead. But for a minute there—''

Erin said softly, ''Sometimes I find myself picking up the phone and dialing my mother's number before I realize she won't be there. I don't think that means I'm crazy. I think it means I still miss her.''

He reached up and touched Erin's hair, combing his fingers through the strands. ''I've never been able to talk to anyone about this before. It feels good.''

Erin was deeply touched. She let him pull her into his arms, and she lay her head on his chest, the deep, steady rhythm of his heart lulling her to sleep. And for the first time in years, she knew she would not wake up lonely.

Chapter Twelve

Nick was gone by the time Erin awakened the next morning, and she might have experienced a crushing disappointment if not for the fact that he'd left a note on her pillow. A note that he'd signed, "Love, Nick." A note in which he'd promised to call her later, and to see her that night.

Erin stretched, feeling a bit like Scarlett O'Hara the morning after, as she languished in bed for a few brief moments, reliving in her memories the night she'd just spent with Nick. Then, realizing she had to get to the lab, she hopped out of bed to shower and dress.

Outside, the day was crisp and sunny, the kind of fall morning that Erin always found invigorating. Or perhaps it was the night before that had put a new spring in her step, brought a secret smile to her lips. Whatever the reason, Erin decided to walk the few blocks to campus.

She'd told Nick about her family, and he hadn't cared. *You aren't responsible for anything your father did,* he'd said. And then he'd confided in her about his own doubts. Their baring of souls had drawn them closer, had made last night anything but a one-night stand.

Last night had been the start of something wonderful for them, the promise of something special. She and Nick were falling in love, and Erin, usually reserved about her personal life, had to fight the urge to shout it to the world.

"I'm in love with Nick Gallagher," she whispered, then glanced around quickly to see if anyone had overheard her. A couple of students stared at her curiously, no doubt chalking her up as the proverbial absent-minded professor chatting to herself.

Across the street, a man sat reading a newspaper on a bench. The light changed, and as Erin started across, he looked up, catching her eye briefly before he went back to his paper. But Erin thought, in that brief instant when their gazes touched, that he looked familiar.

A tingle of alarm stole up her spine, but she was already into the intersection. She kept walking, telling herself that the man was simply someone she'd seen on campus. It was broad daylight, and the traffic was heavy. Surely she was safe on a public street.

But it had only been a few days ago that someone had killed Clive Avery. Slit his throat, then hid his body.

Erin crossed the street, her head slightly lowered, but she sensed the man's gaze on her. When she got to the other side, he stood, blocking her path. Panic bloomed inside her, but somehow he didn't look all that threatening in his expensive business suit, his blond hair clipped short and stylish. His eyes were blue. A very light blue, like Erin's...

"Hello, Irish," he said with a smile.

"How did you...I know you," Erin said on a gasp. She stared at him for a moment as recognition fell into place. "You were at the Gallaghers' last night."

He held out his hand. "My name is Dylan O'Roarke. I'm married to Kaitlin Gallagher."

"O'Roarke?" Erin felt her breath leave her in a painful rush.

"I'm your cousin," he said on another smile.

"I didn't even know I had a cousin," she said in shock. "Why didn't you say something last night?"

"It wasn't the time or place for shocking introductions." His answer seemed strained. He took her arm. "Why don't we sit down? You look a little stunned."

Without protest, Erin let him guide her to the bench. They both sat down, staring at each other. "We look something alike," he said, pleased. "I've often wondered what you looked like."

"You knew me?" Erin asked in confusion. "I'm afraid I don't remember you."

"You were just a baby when you and your mother left. I was two, the same age as Daniel."

At the mention of her brother, Erin's eyes filled with unexpected tears. "How is he? *Where* is he?"

Dylan stared at her in surprise. His brows drew together in a deep scowl. "Are you telling me you don't know what happened to him?"

Her heart hammered suddenly. "He's not—"

"He's alive," Dylan said, his expression hard. "If you can call it living. There's no easy way to tell you this, Erin. Daniel is in prison. He's been on death row for almost eight years."

A chill shot through Erin, the cold more deep and pervasive than anything she'd ever experienced. *"Death row?"* she said in a whisper. "Oh, my God."

Dylan's face grew grave. "He needs you, Erin. Your family needs you."

"Needs me?" she said doubtfully. "What can I do?"

"Then you're willing to help?"

His unfaltering gaze made Erin uneasy. "I don't even know what happened, why he's in prison. I don't know Daniel at all. What makes you think there's anything I can do to help him?"

Dylan's gaze on her deepened. "Have you ever heard of a young woman named Ashley Dallas?"

She knew the name. What was it Mary Alice Stanton had told her? *A man was convicted of her murder, and he's been on death row for several years. Now, however, there's a possibility he may be released.*

The memory made Erin gasp again. Her gaze shot to Dylan.

He nodded gravely. "I see you have heard of her. I'm Daniel's attorney," he said. "It's my job to do whatever I can to get him out of prison."

"Even if he's guilty?"

"He's not."

"How can you be that sure?" Erin asked almost desperately. "He received the death penalty, didn't he? The evidence must have been convincing."

"Oh, it was." The fine lines around Dylan's mouth tightened. "And it was all planted. Daniel was framed, Irish."

"Don't call me that," she all but snapped. "My name is Erin."

"You've remained Irish to us all these years."

She gave him a hard look. "Who is 'us'?"

"Uncle Richard. Daniel. Me. We're just about all that's left of the O'Roarkes. Except, of course, for you."

"I'm not an O'Roarke. My name is Casey," she said coldly.

"Look in the mirror...Erin. Tell me then you're not an O'Roarke."

This couldn't be happening, Erin thought. The whole scene was so surreal. For so many years, she'd wondered secretly about her family, dreamed about them, and now here she was, face-to-face with a cousin she never even knew existed.

"You say he was framed?" she asked reluctantly. "Can you prove it?"

Instead of answering her question, Dylan said pensively, "Maybe I should start at the beginning. I don't know how much your mother may have told you about us, but the O'Roarkes have a rather...colorful history in Chicago, starting when James O'Roarke, our grandfather, immigrated here over seventy years ago from Ireland."

"I know about James O'Roarke," Erin said. "My mother told me all about my grandfather, about his illegal activities."

Dylan cocked his brow slightly. "Did she also tell you about the Gallaghers?"

"The *Gallaghers?* How would my mother know them?"

"Because she was once an O'Roarke. Our grandfather and William Gallagher came over from Ireland together. They were once best friends, but then they fell in love with the same woman."

Erin remembered the sadness in Colleen Gallagher's eyes when she'd said that Erin reminded her of someone she'd once loved very much. James O'Roarke. "What happened?"

"She was engaged to our grandfather, but somehow

William managed to convince her to marry him, instead.''

Erin suspected it wasn't quite as simple as that. ''William Gallagher was a police officer, wasn't he?''

''Yes.''

''And our grandfather was a criminal. Was that why he lost his fiancée to William Gallagher?''

''Our grandfather did some things I'm not proud of,'' Dylan said. ''I'll be the first to admit that. But I'm not sure either of us are in a position to judge him, since we've never known what it was like to go hungry. And worse than that, to watch our family go hungry. Watch our own mother die in childbirth because there wasn't money for a doctor. Watch our baby brother go blind because there wasn't money for an operation.''

''That doesn't excuse what he did.'' But a lump had risen in Erin's throat, and she had a hard time swallowing past it.

''No. But we can understand it, can't we? Our grandfather wasn't all bad, Erin. There was goodness in him. He could be extraordinarily kind, and he always took care of his family. I think you would have liked him.''

Erin closed her eyes briefly. She didn't want to hear this. It was too late to change her perceptions. Too late to make peace with her family.

''For a lot of reasons, we've always hated the Gallaghers, and they've always hated us,'' Dylan continued. ''I grew up believing that anyone named Gallagher was my enemy.''

They've always hated us. Oh, God, Erin thought. No wonder she'd felt a connection with Nick from the first. No wonder she'd sensed that their attraction was somehow taboo.

''Then I met Kaitlin,'' Dylan said.

His tone softened, so much so that Erin couldn't help saying, "You fell in love with her?"

"It was love at first sight," he agreed. "But it took me a while to get over the fact that she was a Gallagher. I had all the preconceived notions about her. I'd been taught that all the Gallaghers were out to get us any way they could. But Kaitlin isn't like that. Her father, on the other hand…"

When he trailed off, Erin said, "What happened to Daniel?"

"Daniel was at the wrong place at the wrong time. He'd always hated the Gallaghers, too, and he and Tony—you probably met him last night—had had a few run-ins before. Daniel got it in his head that if he could take Ashley Dallas away from Tony, it would be some sort of vengeance for everything they'd ever done to us. Maybe he even thought it would be payback for our grandfather.

"Whatever his reason, Daniel went to see Ashley the night she was killed. Evidently she told him that she and Tony were through. Daniel thought that meant he had a chance with her, so he followed her to the party. He and Tony got into a fight, and sometime after that, Ashley left in a huff. Her body was found a few hours later."

"And Daniel?"

"The murder weapon was conveniently found in the bushes near the body. Daniel's fingerprints were on it. Nick's father, Sean, was the one who found the knife."

He was like a hero to me. I always looked up to him.

Erin stared at her cousin in shock. "Are you saying Sean Gallagher somehow planted Daniel's fingerprints on the knife? How? And why?"

"You mean aside from the fact that Daniel was an

O'Roarke?'' His voice was laced with an emotion Erin couldn't quite fathom. ''Daniel's fingerprints were checked against the murder weapon after he was taken into custody. There are ways of transferring fingerprints from one object to another, Erin. You know that.''

But Erin still wasn't buying it. ''Why would Sean Gallagher do that? Why would he risk his reputation to frame Daniel for the murder?''

''Because his own son was at that party. Tony and Ashley were seen in a heated argument before she left. Then Tony disappeared from the party, as well. He says now that he went upstairs and blacked out in his cousin's room, but no one saw him. He couldn't account for his whereabouts at the time of Ashley's murder, but that fact was left out of the official police report.''

Erin felt a migraine pounding at her temples. This was too much to absorb. After last night—

''Are you saying you think Tony Gallagher murdered Ashley Dallas?''

''I don't know,'' Dylan said. ''I do know that critical evidence was left out of the police report by both Sean Gallagher and Ed Dawson. Their motives may not have been any more sinister than trying to protect their own sons, but the end result was that they never looked for the real killer. They railroaded Daniel for a crime he didn't commit.''

Erin sat back against the bench, trying to digest everything Dylan had told her. Did he really believe her brother was innocent? Or was he doing a number on her, playing her for a fool?

She said suspiciously, ''Even if all this is true, why did you come to me with it? There's nothing I can do.''

''You said that before.''

"It's true. This has nothing to do with me."

For the first time, she sensed anger in him, a slow, simmering rage that reminded her suddenly of Nick. "How can you say this has nothing to do with you? We're talking about your brother. You're an O'Roarke, for God's sake."

She rose to leave. "Not anymore. My own father gave me away, remember?"

Dylan stood to face her. "Your mother took you away. She left Daniel behind. How do you think he's dealt with her abandonment all these years?"

She said hesitantly, "But my father *chose* him. He only cared about his son."

"And your mother chose you. At least that's how Daniel always perceived it."

The revelation stunned Erin. Left her reeling. She couldn't say anything for a moment. In all these years, she'd never stopped to consider how her brother had felt when she and her mother left. He'd only been two, hardly more than a baby when they'd left him—abandoned him, he would have thought.

Abandoned him...exactly the way Erin was trying to do now.

She rubbed her temples almost viciously. "Look, all that happened a long time ago. My brother and I both have had to deal with the bargain our parents struck. I'm sorry if he was as hurt and lonely and confused as I was growing up. I'm sorry for a lot of things, but what's done is done. We can't change the way we grew up, and I can't change what happened to my brother."

Dylan gripped her forearms suddenly. "But you have the power to make it right now."

"How?"

His grasp tightened when Erin would have pulled

away. "Why do you think you came to Chicago, Erin?"

"I was offered a wonderful position—" She broke off when she saw the look in his eyes.

"Your father built FAHIL. Uncle Richard arranged for Hillsboro to lure you here, make you an offer you couldn't refuse."

"*Why?*" Erin's heart beat a wild staccato in her chest. She was hardly aware of the traffic, the curious glances from passersby. Her gaze was riveted on her cousin.

"Because he wanted you close. He wanted you back in the family. Once your mother died, he felt he had a chance."

"He knows about my mother's death?"

"He knows everything about you. Where you grew up. The schools you went to. Your first boyfriend. That professor in college," Dylan added softly.

Erin's hand flew to her mouth. "Oh, God. All these years, he's had me followed? He's watched me?"

"He's protected you. Looked out for your best interests. He's very proud of you."

She didn't want to hear any more of this. Couldn't hear any more of it. "I don't believe you. He's sent you here because he needs something from me. What does he want?"

Dylan looked as if he wanted to deny her charge, but then he said, very deliberately, "He's interested in the remains that were recovered in Wisconsin."

Erin's heart plunged to her stomach. A fist of fear tightened inside her chest. "How did you know about that?"

"Richard Gallagher is a powerful man, Erin. He has a lot of contacts."

"Someone in the Webber County Sheriff's Department must have called him." It was a statement, not a question, and Dylan didn't bother to deny it. "Why is he so interested in the remains?"

"Sean Gallagher disappeared from that area eight years ago. The police have always claimed Daniel was their leading suspect. If Sean's body has been recovered, another case against Daniel could be built. Or I should say, fabricated."

Her brother was suspected of killing Nick's father? Erin felt hysteria bubbling inside her. She'd known all along Nick hadn't leveled with her about those remains. She'd guessed that his almost obsessive precautions were because he was building a case against someone important. She just had never suspected that that someone was her own brother.

"How did my father find out about the remains?" she asked Dylan.

"It doesn't matter. What matters now are your conclusions."

Erin stared at Dylan in disbelief. "And you think I'll tell my father what I've found? You think I'll tell him anything? My God, a man was killed after we excavated those remains. We were all almost killed. Was that my father's orders?"

It was Dylan's turn to look astounded. "How could you think your own father would ever have you harmed?"

"Why wouldn't I think that?" Erin said coldly. "He's a criminal, isn't he? A brutal, ruthless man who would do anything to get his only son out of prison. That's why he's come to me after all these years, isn't it? So that I'll compromise my findings. So that I'll protect Daniel."

"You've got it all wrong, Erin. We've come to you to make sure no one else compromises your findings."

"Meaning?"

"You've become close to Nick Gallagher."

"Leave him out of this," Erin said angrily. "He has nothing to do with any of this."

"He has everything to do with this." Dylan's mouth hardened as he gazed down at Erin. "Of all the Gallaghers, Nick is the one who hates us the most. He would do anything to keep Daniel in prison."

"I don't believe that."

"Sean Gallagher deliberately withheld evidence from Daniel's investigation. You think Sean's son isn't capable of duplicity?"

"How can you even ask that? You know him. You're part of his family now."

"I'm married to a Gallagher," Dylan said grimly. "But I will always be an O'Roarke. And so will you, Erin. No matter how much you try to deny it."

NICK'S STOMACH tightened as he stared at his mother. She was sitting in his uncle's office at the south side station, along with Ed Dawson, and from the looks on their faces Nick knew that Liam had come clean about the remains.

Liam said, "Sit down, Nick. We've got a lot to talk about."

Nick remained standing. He walked over to the window, putting a hand briefly on his mother's shoulder as he passed by her. She looked up, her eyes tearless, and smiled at him sadly. But there was something in her expression that resembled neither grief nor accusation. She did, however, appear nervous.

Beside her, Ed Dawson looked the same as always—

cold, remote, in control. He never wore the police uniform as had his predecessors, but instead dressed more like a stockbroker or lawyer. His attire grated on cops like Nick. It was as if Dawson was trying to distance himself from the very department he controlled.

He gave Nick a return appraisal, just as cool. "Some interesting developments," was all he said.

"You'd better explain what's going on," Liam said wearily. He turned to Nick's mother. "I'm sorry I didn't tell you about this when it first came to my attention, Maggie. You had a right to know. Nick and I both should have come to you sooner."

"Why didn't you?" This from Dawson.

Nick saw his uncle visibly flinch, and he knew precisely what was running through Liam's mind. He was due for retirement with full benefits in a couple of years. He didn't need this.

"I thought it was a good idea to keep it quiet until I knew for sure the identity of the remains," Nick explained. "And just for the record, I still don't have a positive ID."

Dawson glanced at him sharply. "Why not?"

"Dr. Casey is working on the remains, but her findings aren't yet conclusive. But the general physical description she's supplied me with so far is a match."

"What about a DNA test?" Dawson asked.

"That's the next step," Nick agreed.

Nick's gaze moved to his mother. She looked a little pale, he thought. He saw her draw a long breath before she slipped her hand inside Dawson's.

"What about cause of death?" she asked softly.

Nick hesitated. "Dr. Casey's preliminary judgment is that the victim—whoever he is—was murdered."

The room fell silent, tomblike, as Nick studied their

faces. They all seemed a little stunned by his words, even though it hardly came as a surprise. They'd all known for years that Sean Gallagher had been murdered. They'd just never had the proof.

"I want to be kept apprised of Dr. Casey's findings," Dawson said at last. "This case is important to me, too, Nick."

"I know." Nick had never liked Ed Dawson, cared for him even less now that he knew the man was involved with his mother. But Dawson had suffered a loss, too, in all this. His stepdaughter was dead, and by all accounts, Dawson had loved Ashley as if she were his own daughter. And now the man who had brutally murdered her was about to be released from prison, unless they could find a way to stop it.

For the first time, Nick allowed himself to imagine what all this had to be like for Superintendent Dawson, the top cop in the city, whose hands were tied just like everyone else's when it came to the courts.

"As soon as I know anything, I'll let you know," Nick assured them.

His mother rose. "I'd like to speak to Nick alone for a moment, please."

Dawson looked as if he wanted to protest, but then, after touching Maggie's arm briefly, he followed Liam from the office, closing the door with a soft click.

Maggie walked over to stand beside Nick. For a moment, they both stared out the dirty window, but neither of them was studying the parking lot below. His mother appeared composed, but Nick suspected that underneath, her turmoil was as great as his.

"How are you holding up through all this?" she asked him softly.

Nick shrugged, his gaze still focused on the asphalt

below. "I'm okay. This just confirms what we always knew."

"But you don't have a positive ID yet. It may not be your father."

Nick glanced at her in surprise. Was she still holding out hope, even after all this time? "Like I said, the general physical description Erin came up with was a match. The remains were found near Dad's cabin. That's pretty concrete, Mom."

"A lot of bodies have been found in those woods," she said almost stubbornly.

"The DNA test will confirm what I already know." He turned to stare down at her. "Why are you having a hard time believing this is Dad? I would think, all things considered, you'd welcome the closure."

She looked a little startled by his remarks. "What are you talking about?"

"I'm talking about Dawson." Nick tried to keep his voice even and nonjudgmental, but his mother glanced up at him with a frown.

She took his hand in both hers. "No one could ever take your father's place."

Nick almost smiled at that. "I'm not a ten year old. I know that. I also know you deserve to have a life. I'm happy for you."

"Nick—" She removed her hand from his and turned to walk over to Liam's desk. For the longest time, she kept her back to him. When she finally faced him, there was a quality in her eyes that gave Nick that same uneasiness he'd felt the other day when he'd sensed she wanted to tell him something. She had something on her mind now, something that was obviously eating away at her.

He walked over and put his hands on her shoulders. "What is it? What's bothering you?"

Her eyes suddenly flooded with tears. "Nick, Nick." She put her hand to his cheek. "When I think how close you and Sean used to be..."

Nick's throat tightened. "It's okay. Nothing can ever change that."

She closed her eyes briefly. "He loved his family so much. Everything he did was for us. He always tried to protect us."

"I know that."

"Just don't ever forget it," his mother whispered. "Hold on to that, Nick. No matter what."

ERIN FINALLY got up from the bench and walked across the campus toward the FAHIL building. It was probably her imagination, she told herself, but she could feel someone watching her. Was her cousin lurking somewhere nearby? Her father? One of his minions?

Erin thought about that afternoon several days ago when Ross had told her he'd seen a stranger outside the building who appeared to be waiting for her. She wondered now if that man had been sent by her father to keep secret tabs on her, just as he had done all her life.

Or had he? Did she really believe that her father had had any interest in her back then? That he had kept track of her life and her career? That he had built this lab for her?

Or was his interest in her a recent development, triggered solely by the fact that she was now in a unique position to help Daniel? If her findings concluded that Case 00-04 was not Sean Gallagher, or that he had not been murdered, then there was a good chance Daniel could walk from prison a free man, without fear of another conviction.

Erin's heart began to beat in slow, painful jerks as she considered all the possibilities. Her father was a powerful man, and, according to her mother, brutal and ruthless. Was it possible he'd engineered Clive Avery's death? Nick had said Avery once lived in Chicago, that he'd been a CPD officer. What if he had known Richard O'Roarke back then? What if he'd been on her father's payroll all this time?

Nick's voice seemed to taunt her. *He served his usefulness, then he was another piece of evidence that had to be gotten rid of.*

And Dylan O'Roarke asserting: *Of all the Gallaghers, Nick is the one who hates us the most, Erin. He would do anything to keep Daniel in prison.*

Erin had the childish notion that if she put her hands to her ears, she could stop all those voices. All these doubts. But that wouldn't work, and she knew it. The voices were screaming at her too loudly.

Sean Gallagher deliberately withheld evidence from Daniel's investigation. You think Sean's son isn't capable of duplicity?

...I'd do just about anything to put a murderer back where he belongs.

...I will always be an O'Roarke. And so will you, Erin. No matter how much you try to deny it.

...I think we had something back there, a moment when things could have worked out for us. But I'm thinking now that we may have lost it somehow.

"HEY, NICK, I got the information you were looking for."

Nick glanced up from the file he'd been studying.

Donald Glock, the station's computer expert, held a sheath of printouts in his pudgy hands as he hovered in Nick's doorway. "You know, that license plate number you gave me?"

An image of the black Mercedes he'd seen outside the FAHIL offices yesterday flashed through Nick's mind. He closed the file and motioned Donald inside. "What'd you find out?"

Donald situated himself carefully in the chair across from Nick's desk. Officer Glock liked his doughnuts, and his butt was starting to show it. "Like I told you yesterday, the car was registered to a corporation. Wellstone Limited."

"You said it was some sort of import-export business."

Donald nodded. "Right. But they're a subsidiary of a larger corporation, Emerald Isle Enterprises—EIE. They own a fleet of ships, among other things, and appear to be on the up-and-up. Tax records check out, all that sort of thing. But when I called up a list of their board of directors, that's when things started getting interesting."

Nick glanced at him sharply. "Interesting how?"

"The chairman of the board is none other than Richard O'Roarke."

Nick felt his nerve endings quicken. This could very well be the break he'd been waiting for, the connection to the O'Roarkes he'd been hoping for. That black Mercedes had been parked outside the FAHIL building after his father's remains had been brought there, and Nick would be willing to bet a month's pay that that same car was the one that had followed him and Erin two nights ago.

The O'Roarkes were getting careless. Or desperate.

Sooner or later, one of them would slip up. Give themselves away. And when that happened, Nick would be ready. Maybe he could nail Daniel and Richard both, put the whole damn O'Roarke clan away for good this time.

Meanwhile, however, he worried about Erin. The O'Roarkes were only too aware of the importance of the remains at FAHIL. Clive Avery was dead because of those remains. Nick didn't want Erin to be the O'Roarkes' next victim.

Because when all this was over, when he'd settled the score with the O'Roarkes in a way he could live with, Nick had every intention of making Erin a permanent fixture in his life. Assuming, of course, she felt the same way about him.

And after last night, he had reason to believe that she did. He felt his body respond to the memory, and he tried to stop thinking about it. Tried to put Erin out of his mind, but it wasn't easy because he couldn't wait to see her again. Couldn't wait to make love to her again. Couldn't wait to tell her how he felt about her.

He was in love with her, and he had been, Nick suspected, since that first night in her lab, when he'd glimpsed how much she cared about her work, when he'd witnessed firsthand what a rare and beautiful soul she possessed.

But even more important was the fact that he knew he could trust her. To a cop, trust meant everything.

WHEN SHE REACHED her office, Erin closed the door and sat down wearily at her desk. Why should she care about any of this? she asked herself sternly. Why did Nick ever have to find out who she was? She was Erin Casey now. She had no connection to the O'Roarkes, no loyalty, no anything. She hadn't seen Daniel since she was nine months old, since their father had agreed to give her up so he could keep his only son.

You aren't responsible for anything your father did.

Nick had said that himself, but the logic couldn't dispel the nausea eating at Erin's stomach. Dylan was right. O'Roarke blood ran in her veins, and nothing could ever change that fact.

Turning on her computer, Erin logged on to the Internet, surprised by how many hits her search engine turned up for Sean Gallagher. Limiting the search by adding the name Ashley Dallas, she pinpointed the sites that dealt with the young woman's death and Sean Gallagher's subsequent disappearance.

After almost an hour, she sat stunned by what she'd learned.

No wonder she'd felt such a sense of foreboding with Nick. They were tied together in ways neither one of them had known about. Or had he known?

Was it possible that Nick had sought her out because he'd somehow found out who she really was? Was he trying to use her in some way? Was that what last night was really all about?

No, that didn't make sense. He'd said he wanted her examination of the remains to be without compromise, and if he'd found out who she was, she would have been the last person he would have come to for help. Her relationship to the O'Roarkes could seriously jeopardize the case he was building.

The case against her brother.

Erin put a hand to her mouth, her mind whirling. What should she do now? Tell Nick everything and remove herself from the case? But if he knew she was an O'Roarke, if *anyone* knew, her credibility could be irrevocably damaged. She might never again be able to practice in her chosen field, and Erin's work meant everything to her.

What if she said nothing? She wasn't an O'Roarke anymore. She was Dr. Erin Casey, legally and in every other way that counted. She knew she could examine the remains in her lab, reach her conclusions without any bias whatsoever for one simple reason—bones didn't lie.

Chapter Thirteen

Dylan O'Roarke was waiting for Erin at the same bench that afternoon as she walked home from work. When she first saw him, she had an almost overwhelming urge to turn and run the other way. Before this morning, telling Nick she was an O'Roarke would have been difficult, but now it was impossible. Not only was her integrity on the line, but her cousin's claim that she was in a position to make sure evidence wasn't contaminated bore heavily on her shoulders. Was it possible someone might try to interfere with her findings? Was it possible the Gallaghers could hate her family that much?

She wouldn't do this, Erin resolved. She wouldn't let Dylan O'Roarke's innuendoes plant her mind with doubts about Nick and his family. After all, she knew Nick better than she knew her brother, didn't she? Daniel *could* be a murderer for all Erin knew. Why should she risk everything for him?

Because she wanted almost desperately to believe he wasn't guilty, Erin realized suddenly. But even if she came to be convinced of Daniel's innocence, Nick never would be. Her brother—and her birth name—would always be a wedge between them.

Dylan stood as she approached. "How are you?"

"How do you expect me to be?" she said glumly, "After the bombshell you dropped on me this morning."

"It's a difficult situation for you, I realize."

"How do you do it?" she asked him almost desperately.

He cocked a brow. "Do what?"

"You're an O'Roarke and you're married to a Gallagher. Aren't your loyalties constantly divided?"

"Sometimes." He paused. "You're talking about Nick." When she didn't answer, he said softly, "Are you in love with him?"

Erin shook her head sadly. "I don't know. Maybe. I care about him. But I don't know how he'd react if he found out who I am—was."

"Don't you mean *when* he finds out?"

"Why should he have to know?" she asked almost angrily. "I'm not an O'Roarke anymore. My name is Erin Casey."

"How many times have you told yourself that over the years? Have you ever once made yourself believe it?"

"What do you really want from me?" she asked bitterly. "What does my father want?"

Dylan's smile flashed again. An O'Roarke smile. The same smile Erin saw in her own pictures. "Right now, he wants to see you."

THE GATES swung open, and the black Mercedes swept through with hardly more than a whisper of sound. Erin glanced over her shoulder as the gates closed behind them, and a panicky sensation engulfed her. What was she doing here? How had she allowed Dylan O'Roarke to persuade her into an interview with her father? Richard O'Roarke was the embodiment of all her childhood fears, and along with the panic came a sharp prick of guilt. Her mother would not have wanted this.

It was almost as if Madeline's spirit was there in the back seat of the limo with her, whispering the warnings in Erin's ear. *Your father is an evil man, Erin. An evil man born of an evil man. You are well out of his life.*

Massive oak trees, displaying breathtaking fall hues that ranged from pale apricot to burnt orange, hugged the winding drive, and as the woods thinned, Erin got her first glimpse of the house. The fading light glinted off the windows, creating a twinkling effect that almost seemed surreal. The place was even grander than Erin had imagined, but not at all ostentatious. The ivy-trimmed redbrick facade was both elegant and inviting, emanating an old-world charm totally at odds with the mausoleum Erin had erected in her mind.

So this was the home her grandfather, James O'Roarke, had built some seventy years ago with money he'd made from bootlegging. Later, his other ill-gotten gains had provided additions to the original house, the formal gardens, and a collection of artwork her mother had once told Erin was worthy of a museum.

Richard, James's oldest son, had inherited the house, but the business, which included a vast conglomerate of shipping interests, had been divided equally between the two sons—Richard, and his brother, Michael, who was Dylan's father, now deceased.

As they approached the house, Erin realized she knew more about the O'Roarke family history than she'd realized. Her mother had never kept Erin's heritage a secret. When she'd asked questions, Madeline had answered, but there had always been a caveat: Stay away from the O'Roarkes.

Only when Erin had questioned her mother about Daniel, had Madeline's expression softened. She would look so unhappy at times that Erin had learned at an early age never to mention her brother's name. It wasn't so difficult to pretend he didn't exist. After all, Daniel was someone Erin had never known, a stranger who shared her parents but nothing else.

As Erin grew older, her mother had become more melancholy. They'd remained close until her death, but Erin had always known there was a part of Madeline's life she didn't share. There was a bit of her mother's heart she could never lay claim to.

In Erin's final college days, still living at home, she'd often heard her mother weeping at night, when she'd thought Erin was asleep. Looking back, she realized her mother must have found out about Daniel, that he'd been tried and convicted of murder and sent to death row. She must have been blaming herself for not being able to save him as she had Erin.

Guilt pierced Erin again, but this time it was for her brother. In all these years, Erin had not once tried to contact him. She'd managed to convince herself she'd only been respecting her mother's wishes, but Erin realized now that her reluctance to seek out her brother was a much deeper issue. A part of her had secretly resented him, because he'd been their father's chosen one. Erin had always wondered if, given the same choice, her mother would have taken Daniel away instead of Erin.

The car stopped, and the driver got out to open the door for them. Dylan took Erin's arm. "Nervous?"

She shrugged. "Why should I be?" But of course she was.

Dylan looked as if he wanted to say more, but instead, he ushered her up the front steps to the double oak doors and rang the bell. Almost instantly one of the doors was drawn back to reveal a slender blond maid who smiled shyly when she saw Dylan and Erin.

"Mr. O'Roarke is waiting for you in the study." She led them across the polished teak floor of the foyer, down a long hallway lined with gilt-framed paintings, to another set of double doors which she slid open. She stood back for them to enter first, then said, "Can I get you something to drink?"

"Nothing for me," Erin said quickly.

But Dylan flashed her a charming grin. "I wouldn't say no to a cup of your tea, Meghan."

The woman ducked her head demurely. "Of course. Anything else, sir?"

"That'll be all for now, Meghan, thank you," said a cultured voice from across the room.

Erin had thought the study empty when she and Dylan had first entered. The huge bookcases—not neat and orderly as one might have expected in such a home, but overflowing and untidy from much use—had caught her attention immediately, and she hadn't noticed the gray-haired man sitting in a leather chair by the fire.

He rose now, tall and stately, his eyes, even from a distance, light blue and very clear. O'Roarke eyes, Erin had come to realize.

She wasn't sure what she'd been expecting. Marlon Brando from *The Godfather*? James Cagney in his gangster role days? An older, but no less intimidating Robert DeNiro?

More than anything, Richard O'Roarke reminded Erin of an aging college professor, a man most in his element when surrounded by his books.

Slightly taken aback by his presence, Erin realized she was staring. She glanced away awkwardly, asking herself again why she had come here.

"Uncle Richard, this is Erin," Dylan said softly. He took Erin's elbow, urging her forward, but before she could cross the room, Richard came to her.

He moved with quiet ease, the way of a man who neither craved attention nor shied away from it. He reached for her hand, clasping it warmly in both of his, and for a moment, Erin wondered if her mother had been lying to her all those years. This man was no monster. Actually, he seemed quite charming.

But then, as he smiled down at her, Erin saw a hint of cruelty in his mouth, a subtle arrogance in the way he studied her. A wolf in sheep's clothing.

She removed her hand from his, and a brief frown flashed across his brow. What had he expected? Erin thought. That his warmth and charm could wash away the bargain he'd struck twenty-nine years ago?

"Come and sit by the fire," he said almost formally. "Dylan, would you mind giving us a few minutes alone?"

"I'll just go have my tea in the kitchen with Meghan," he said cheerfully.

Erin wanted to clutch at her cousin's arm and keep him from going, but before she could move a muscle, he strode from the room and slid the doors closed behind him. She and her father were alone together for the first time in nearly thirty years.

She took a deep breath as she turned to face him. He'd moved back to his chair by the hearth, and the warmth of the fire softened his mouth. The cruelty she'd glimpsed early might only have been an illusion. But it wasn't.

Reluctantly, Erin joined him by the fire and seated herself in the chair he indicated.

"You look like the O'Roarkes," he said after a moment. "Though you have your mother's complexion. Maddie always had the most beautiful skin."

Maddie? He'd called her mother Maddie? His tone sounded almost...fond.

Don't be fooled by his charm, her mother's voice seemed to warn her.

"Why did you want to see me?" Erin blurted.

His eyes flickered with an emotion she couldn't define. "You're my daughter."

"I've been your daughter for twenty-nine years," she pointed out. "You made no effort to see me before."

"Because I had an agreement with your mother." If there was regret in his tone, Erin didn't hear it.

"Yes, I know all about that bargain. The only way you'd agree to give Mother a divorce was if she gave you sole custody of Daniel. In return, you gave up any legal claim to me."

"Your mother could be a very unreasonable woman," he said with regret.

Erin glanced at him, knowing his amiable demeanor was only a facade. Inside beat a heart as cold and cruel as the grave. "How was *she* unreasonable? You gave her no choice. You made it clear you would never give up your son, and she knew there was no way she could fight your money and your power for him. So she saved the only child she could, the daughter you had no interest in. Unreasonable?" Erin gave him a cold, disparaging glance. "My mother was the most selfless woman I've ever known."

"And yet she walked away from her son without a backward glance."

A wave of rage swept over Erin. She rose and stood staring down at him. "How dare you speak of my mother that way? I won't listen to it. I won't listen to another word you have to say." She whirled toward the door, but his next words stopped her cold.

"Even if it means saving your brother's life? Your own flesh and blood?"

She closed her eyes briefly before turning to face him. "I can't help Daniel. There's nothing I can do for him."

"You're wrong, Irish. You're the only one who can help him."

The anger inside her faded as she stared down at her father, and the apprehension she'd experienced earlier tingled along her spine. Here was a man she'd been taught all her life to fear. A man who would do anything—perhaps even sacrifice his own daughter—to save his son. Had he committed murder for Daniel? Was he responsible for Clive Avery's death?

She shivered in the warm glow of the fireplace. "There's nothing I can do," she said again.

Her father rose to face her. When he moved to take her arms, she backed away from him. Something quick and frightening flashed in his blue eyes. The same eyes Erin saw in the mirror.

"What conclusions have you reached about the remains that were taken to your lab?"

"My work is confidential."

He waved a dismissive hand, as if his patience with her was coming to an end. "Can you prove Sean Gallagher was murdered?'' His voice was hard, relentless, the voice of a man with a lot of power and the willingness to use it.

Erin shivered again. ''I won't change my findings,'' she warned him. ''I won't compromise my integrity.''

He looked at her incredulously. ''Not even to save your own brother's life?''

''If he's guilty, he deserves to be in prison.''

''But he's not guilty. He was railroaded by the Gallaghers, and now they're trying to do the same thing to him again. Can't you see that, girl?''

She lifted her chin at his tone. ''Why would they do that?''

''To save one of their own, maybe. Or maybe to get back at us. They've been on our backs for years,'' he all but spat.

''And why would they be on your back,'' Erin demanded, ''if you haven't done anything wrong?''

Richard gave her a long, measured look. ''Maddie did a real number on you, didn't she?''

''She told me the truth about my family,'' Erin said. ''She never wanted me to be a part of it.''

''She saw to that, didn't she?'' he muttered bitterly. His shoulders slumped a bit as he turned to stare into the fire. ''Our businesses are legitimate, and have been for years.''

Erin doubted that. She said coolly, ''That wasn't always the case, was it?''

''Your grandfather came to this country without a nickel in his pocket. His mother and father were both dead, and his younger siblings had no one else to count on. They were starving back in Ireland. He did what he had to do to save them.''

''So he became a criminal.''

Something that might have been sorrow flickered over her father's features, but it was gone so quickly, Erin wondered if she'd only imagined it. Still, she regretted her harsh words. Her grandfather was dead after all. She hadn't even known him. It was not her place to pass judgment.

"I'm sorry," she said softly. "I shouldn't have said that about your father."

He gave her a cynical smile. "I'm sure you've said worse about your own father."

His words tore at her defenses, and she regretted not just her harsh words, but the way she'd pulled away from him. She couldn't remember ever having been embraced by this man, and now, standing before him, even knowing what she knew about him and suspecting much worse, Erin realized that she longed to have his arms around her. She yearned to feel the bond with him that only fathers and daughters could feel.

Her throat tight, she said, "Did you really have FAHIL built?"

His mouth hardened. "Dylan shouldn't have told you."

"Why?"

He shook his head. "That was my present to you. Finding out I was responsible tarnishes it."

"Did you think I couldn't earn a lab of my own?"

He looked genuinely surprised by that. "My God, no. You're brilliant. Any lab in the country would have had you. I wanted you here, in Chicago. With your mother gone, I thought you might need me."

A rush of emotion swept over Erin. Tears stung her eyes, but she forced them back, reminding herself that she'd managed just fine on her own. Still...

"I don't know if I believe you," she said slowly. "I

don't know if I can trust you. But I do know this. I won't compromise my findings. Not for you, not even for Daniel.''

"And what about for Nick Gallagher?"

The question shocked her. "What do you mean?"

"Would you compromise your integrity for him?"

Erin stared at her father sadly. "That you would even ask me that question proves how very little you know about me."

THE BIG, black Mercedes pulled to the curb in front of Erin's apartment, and the driver got out to open the door for her. Erin climbed out, feeling a bit like Alice in Wonderland as she murmured her thanks. Dylan got out, too, and bent to kiss her cheek.

"Thank you for coming, Erin. At least now you know Uncle Richard isn't the ogre you seemed to think he was."

To be honest, Erin wasn't sure what to make of her visit with her father. One moment he seemed charming and relaxed, the next intense and dictatorial. She wasn't at all convinced her mother had been dead wrong about him. Perhaps Madeline, in her heartbreak over the divorce and leaving her son, had exaggerated Richard's cruelty. Then again, maybe she hadn't. That was a conclusion Erin would have to reach on her, she supposed.

"See you soon?"

Erin shrugged noncommittally as she watched her cousin climb back into the Mercedes, and the huge car sped off.

She stood shivering a little in the stiff breeze, watching the glow of the taillights. The sound of a car door slamming across the street startled her into alertness, and Erin spun, her heart accelerating.

"Nick?" She felt a rush of pleasure as she recognized him, but then, as he came to stand next her, she knew instinctively something was wrong. His expression, even in the streetlight, looked angry.

"Where've you been, Erin?" The question was casually spoken, but Erin detected a subtle edge that might have been suspicion.

Apprehension tugged at her. "What?"

"I asked where'd you been. Who you've been with."

She tried to shrug off his questions. "Are you interrogating me, Nick?"

"No." He took a step toward her, his face enigmatic in the streetlight. "I only have two questions for you. How do you know Richard O'Roarke? What were you doing in his car?"

So he knew. She glanced up at him, realizing with a sinking feeling in her stomach that she hadn't imagined the anger.

"Richard O'Roarke is my father, Nick."

She saw a shock wave roll over his features, followed closely by disbelief, then the anger again. "You're an *O'Roarke*?"

Slowly, she nodded. "My mother took me away when I was just a baby. As I told you last night, she had our names legally changed to protect me."

"Because your father was dangerous."

Again Erin nodded.

"Then what were you doing with him?" He reached for her, then let his arm fall back to his side. "If you believe what your mother told you, why were you in Richard O'Roarke's car?"

"Because I went to see him tonight. He's still my

father,'' Erin tried to explain. ''Can you blame me for being curious?''

''No.'' Nick gazed down at her in the streetlight. They'd been so close last night, Erin thought. As close as two people could be. Now he seemed a million miles away, and all because her name had once been O'Roarke. All because she'd gone to see her father tonight. ''What I blame you for is not telling me.''

''Can we go inside?'' She spread her hands in supplication. ''I think we need to talk about this.''

Wordlessly he followed her up the stairs and waited while she unlocked her door. Once inside, she flicked on a light and turned off her alarm. Macavity came out of the shadows, blinking in the sudden light. He rubbed against Erin's legs, demanding attention. She bent and absently smoothed the fur on his head for a moment before straightening to face Nick.

His expression, if possible, was even more closed. He stood rigidly in her tiny living room, hands shoved in his pockets, and Erin couldn't help contrasting again the difference between last night and now.

''I'm sorry I didn't tell you,'' she said. ''But I honestly didn't think it was important. My name is Erin Casey now. That's who I am. I didn't know until this morning that our families have been at war all these years. I didn't even know my own brother was in prison, or that you suspect the remains we excavated are your father's. Why didn't *you* tell me?''

''Because I wanted your findings to be uncompromised, but that's impossible now,'' Nick said bitterly.

''Why is it impossible? Bones don't lie, Nick. They tell me what they tell me no matter who my father and brother are. No matter who *your* father is. No matter what our families have done to each other. The fact that I was born an O'Roarke doesn't change anything.''

"It changes everything, Erin. You can't be that naive. Surely you realize that as an expert witness, your credibility would be seriously challenged—by both the defense and the prosecution.''

"You can have another anthropologist examine the remains.''

"Too late. They've been in your care this whole time.''

Erin didn't like what he seemed to be implying. "Are *you* challenging my credibility, Nick? Are you suggesting I may have tampered with evidence?''

He scrubbed his face with both his hands. "Don't you see what's happened here? We've both compromised our integrity by what we did last night.''

His words stung her. "Last night, you said there was no reason we couldn't see each other. No reason we couldn't be involved.''

"Last night, I didn't know who you were.''

"Which is the bigger obstacle here, Nick?'' she asked with her own bitter edge. "The fact that a case has been jeopardized or that my last name was once O'Roarke?''

He didn't say anything for a moment, but turned instead to walk over to the window, staring out. When he finally glanced back at her, his face looked grim. "Your brother is a murderer, Erin. He killed Ashley Dallas, and I have every reason to believe he killed my father. I can't let him walk. You do understand that, don't you?''

"I understand that this is a complicated case.''

He turned to her. "Complicated how?''

"Let me ask you something.'' She paused, treading

carefully. "What makes you so sure my brother killed your father? You've found no physical evidence, have you?"

"No," Nick agreed. "Not yet."

"What do you mean, not yet?" Erin hated the fact that her cousin had planted even an inkling of doubt about Nick's motives, but now that it was there, Erin couldn't seem to dispel it. After all, how well did she really know him?

Well enough to be in love with him, a little voice reminded her.

"There's always evidence, Erin. There's no such thing as a perfect murder."

"But eight years is a long time."

"There's no statute of limitations on murder. I'll get my father's killer," he said in a voice that chilled her to the bone. "Even if it takes another eight years."

Of all the Gallaghers, Nick is the one who hates us the most, Erin. He would do anything to keep Daniel in prison.

"But what if you're wrong about Daniel?" Erin asked softly. "What if he didn't kill your father? What if he didn't kill Ashley Dallas?"

Nick strode across the room suddenly, taking her arms in both his hands. His eyes were darker than she'd ever seen them. Dark and more than a little menacing. "What are you trying to say?"

"Evidence was withheld in the investigation, wasn't it? What if that evidence could have cleared Daniel?"

"It wouldn't have."

"How can you be so sure? No one saw Daniel kill Ashley."

"His fingerprints were the only ones on the murder weapon."

"They could have been planted."

"By whom?" When Erin didn't answer, Nick's gaze on her narrowed. His grasp tightened slightly. "By whom, Erin?"

She shrugged. "I'm not accusing anyone. I'm merely trying to look at all the facts. From what I've read, your brother had as much a motive for killing Ashley Dallas as mine did."

Erin could tell that it was only sheer force of will that battled the rage welling inside him. His mouth hardened and he dropped his hold on her to clench his fists at his sides. "They've gotten to you, haven't they?"

"No one's gotten to me," she said angrily. "I'm my own person. I draw my own conclusions. There were inconsistencies in Daniel's case and you know it. I'm just asking you to be fair."

"Was your brother fair when he stabbed Ashley Dallas to death? Was he fair when he killed my father?"

"How can you be so sure he did all those things?" Erin asked almost desperately.

Nick glared down at her for a long, tense moment before he turned and strode toward the door. Then he turned and said over his shoulder, "Because he's an O'Roarke, Erin. It's as simple as that."

Chapter Fourteen

Erin knew that it was no use trying to sleep that night, so after showering and changing, she got in her car and headed back to the lab. The sooner she finished her examination of Case 00-04, the better off they'd all be. She was certain Nick would want to transfer the remains to another lab as soon as possible, and deep down, she didn't really blame him. But the fact that he'd questioned her integrity still smarted. There was no way she would ever sabotage her own findings, not even for her own brother.

Not even for Nick.

The corridors in the George Augustine Natural Sciences Building were dark and a bit spooky, and as Erin rode the elevator to the third floor, uneasiness gripped her. She shouldn't have come here. A week ago, she would have thought nothing of working alone in the lab well into the night, but after Clive Avery's murder, she'd been trying to take precautions, just as she had in Knoxville.

In truth, though, she was probably safer inside the than any place in the city. And at work, her hands her mind would be kept busy. She'd have little time for dwelling on the possible damage done to her fledgling relationship with Nick.

Surely he couldn't hold it against her that she'd been born an O'Roarke. Surely he couldn't be that insensitive, but her cousin's warning kept rolling through her mind. *Of all the Gallaghers, Nick is the one who hates us the most.*

Erin tried to tell herself that if he was that kind of man, she wanted nothing more to do with him anyway. But it was more complicated than that and she knew it. She hadn't been raised an O'Roarke, but even so, the short time she'd spent with her father had produced confusing and conflicting emotions. She felt a tug of loyalty in spite of herself, and she understood, even if she couldn't condone, Nick's strong feelings toward her family. When her father had talked about the Gallaghers, a part of Erin had wanted to believe him. Wanted to be convinced that her brother had been railroaded by her family's enemies. She wanted to believe, almost desperately, that Daniel was innocent.

So was that her real reason for coming here? Erin wondered. Because part of her had heeded her father's warning that the Gallaghers—or someone—might compromise evidence in order to keep her brother in prison?

Stepping off the elevator, she started to turn off the alarm and motion detectors, but the system had already been disengaged, which meant someone had either forgotten to turn it on earlier, or else someone was working late in the lab.

She hesitated, uncertain whether or not to investigate further. The contents of the lab—including the remains—were her responsibility, and in spite of her uneasiness, she knew she should make sure nothing was amiss. But as she moved toward the door, a sound behind her startled her, and she whirled, her hand flying to her chest.

Ralph, the security guard, stepped tentatively from a small utility room near the elevator. When he saw that it was Erin, he smiled sheepishly. "Dr. Casey! You gave me a fright! I didn't think anyone was still around."

He had the rumpled look of someone who had been curled up sleeping. Erin wondered if he had a cot tucked away in that utility room. "I just came by to do a little work," she told him. "When I saw that the alarm was turned off, I got a little concerned."

Ralph walked over beside her, scratching the back of his head. "Matter of fact, it was turned off when I came down here to make my rounds. Dr. Quay was here a little while ago. Guess he forgot to turn it on when he left."

Erin frowned. Russell Quay had been working in the lab after hours? He hadn't gotten permission to do so, which was a breach of Erin's security procedures and set a bad example for the rest of the FAHIL staff. And worse, not rearming the alarm system reflected badly on her.

Maybe that was the whole point, she thought. Maybe Russell was purposefully trying to make her look bad.

"Okay, thanks, Ralph," she said. "I'll just check and make sure everything in the lab is in order."

He nodded. "If you need anything, I'll be upstairs checking the offices."

He waited until Erin had inserted her key into the lock, then, with a wave, he stepped into the elevator. Erin opened the door and entered the lab, hesitating for a moment before turning on the lights. She knew this lab like the back of her hand, every shadow, every nook and crevice. There was a strange aroma in the air, a scent that subtly mingled with the disinfectants.

A shiver traced up Erin's spine as she reached for the light switch. It took her eyes a moment to adjust to the brilliance, then, with a gasp, she saw Russell Quay lying on the floor of the lab, blood leaking from a wound at his temple.

"Dr. Quay! Russell!" Erin's heart pounded as she rushed toward him. She thought he was dead, he lay so still. But as she dropped to the floor beside him to feel for a pulse, he groaned. "Dr. Quay, can you hear me? What happened?"

Another groan, but he was still unconscious. As Erin rose and hurried toward the phone, she noticed that the X-ray room door was ajar. She hesitated, feeling the hair at the back of her neck rise. She knew, instinctively, that she and Russell weren't alone.

Before she had time to draw a breath, a man stepped around the door and came toward her. He tossed a gasoline can aside, and it landed with a jarring *clang* in the silence. Several things raced simultaneously through Erin's brain. The fact that he had a gun in his hand. The fact that he'd doused the X-ray room with gasoline. The fact that he intended to burn down the lab in order to destroy Sean Gallagher's remains.

"You picked a bad night to work late, Erin," Ed Dawson told her.

Her heart thundered in her ears as her gaze went from the gun, back to his cold, cold eyes. "What are you doing here? What did you do to Dr. Quay?"

He smiled thinly. "Your concern for Russell Quay is sadly misplaced, I'm afraid. When I approached him he was most enthusiastic about discussing your lack of qualifications for heading up FAHIL.''

"He let you into the lab?"

"Eagerly."

She tried to quell the panic rising inside her, the little voice that whispered she might be dealing with a madman here. But Ed Dawson didn't look crazy. He looked coldly detached, a professional. A man who would do what he had to do to protect himself. But from what?

"What are you doing here?" she asked him again.

"What does it look like I'm doing?" he said sharply. "I'm getting rid of evidence. Destroying anything that might tie me to Sean Gallagher's murder."

Erin's panic turned to terror. Ed Dawson had killed Sean Gallagher? The superintendent of the Chicago Police Department was a murderer?

"No one would ever have known if those remains hadn't been discovered," he said grimly. "If you hadn't been so good at your job, Dr. Casey. But you wouldn't rest until you found out everything, would you? You'd keep digging and digging until you'd know everything there was to know about those remains. Including the fact that I was the one who shot Sean."

Shot? The fear inside Erin subsided for a moment as her mind raced. Dawson had *shot* Sean Gallagher? Case 00-04 had almost certainly been strangled, not shot. Which meant that these remains weren't Sean's. But Dawson had no way of knowing that, because Erin hadn't yet written her report. No one knew of her findings but Nick.

Dawson had assumed the remains were Sean's because of where they'd been recovered. He'd assumed the victim had been shot because he'd used a gun to kill Sean.

"Why did you kill him?" she managed calmly. If she could work her way back to the door...

Sensing her intention, Dawson moved slowly toward her, stalking her. "He was on to me. Or at least, he had his suspicions."

He had no intention of letting Erin walk out of here alive. By stumbling upon him in the lab, she already knew too much. Now he seemed intent on making his confession complete, because he knew she would not be repeating what she heard. Dead men told no tales, but Erin knew that wasn't true. Bones talked loud and clear. Someone would find out what happened, but unfortunately, it would be too late for Erin and for Russell Quay.

"You killed Ashley, too, didn't you?" It was a wild guess, but Erin could see at once that she'd hit on the truth. "And Clive Avery."

A mask of rage descended over Dawson's features. "Ashley played me for a fool, leading me on, making me think she cared for me, while all along she was sleeping with all those other men. *Boys,*" he said spitefully. "Young enough to be my sons. Avery saw me at the cabin and recognized me, so I had to kill him."

His businesslike tone chilled Erin. "How did you plant Daniel O'Roarke's fingerprints on the murder weapon?"

Dawson's gaze suddenly narrowed, regarding her coolly. "O'Roarke came over to our home that night looking for Ashley. The knife must have fallen out of his pocket, because I found it in the chair he'd been sitting in after he left. He wanted Ashley, too. I could see the desire in his eyes when she touched him—" His voice broke, and he struggled for a moment to regain his composure. "She tried to ruin me, the cruel little bitch. She threatened to tell her mother that I'd…touched her inappropriately, made passes at her when we both knew she'd been asking for it all along.''

Oh, God, Erin thought. *Oh, my God.* He'd molested Ashley. Erin saw it so clearly. He'd molested her, and when she'd threatened to blow the whistle on him, he'd killed her with Daniel's knife.

She'd thought earlier that day that she'd glimpsed coldness in her own father's eyes. Maybe even a hint of cruelty. But it was nothing compared to the look she saw in Ed Dawson's eyes.

Without thinking, Erin spun and lunged for the door, but Dawson was on her before she could pull the heavy panel open. He hit her with the gun, viciously, in the back of the head, and Erin's world exploded in pain as she silently slipped to the floor.

NICK STOOD at the top of the stairs outside Erin's apartment and wondered where she'd gone off to. It had taken him less than ten minutes after he'd gone home to his empty apartment to realize what a jerk he'd been, another ten minutes to convince himself that what he and Erin had was worth fighting for no matter what, another ten minutes to race back to her apartment only to find her gone.

He didn't like this. Not after everything that had happened at the cabin. His main concern should have been in protecting Erin, but instead, he'd questioned her integrity. Questioned the motives of a woman who had never given him any reason to doubt her—except for the fact that she was an O'Roarke.

The doubts began to niggle at him again. Why hadn't she told him? Had she really only found out that morning about the feud that had raged between their two families for more than seven decades? Had she really not known that the Gallaghers and the O'Roarkes were mortal enemies?

Had she been completely unaware that she had the power to clear her own brother of Sean Gallagher's murder?

Nick didn't like thinking what he was thinking, but the facts were what they were. Erin was an O'Roarke, and even though she might not be aware of it herself, her loyalties were bound to be tested. And now, because of who she was, his case against Daniel O'Roarke had been all but destroyed. Whatever evidence the bones had contained had been, in effect, tainted because she had been born an O'Roarke.

His resolve hardened. He shouldn't have come here after all. He'd been wrong to question Erin's integrity, but he'd also been wrong in thinking the two of them could work this out. No matter what happened now, he could never be sure of her loyalty. He could never be certain that her findings hadn't been compromised, even if unintentionally.

And if his father's murderer walked free…

Nick's thoughts broke off as he saw a red glow in the sky, coming from the direction of the university. And as dread descended over him, he heard the sirens.

ERIN AWOKE in total darkness. Her head throbbed painfully, and as she reached to touch the wound, her hand skimmed against something over her. She put both hands up, in front of her, and felt along the solid surface. She was lying in some sort of enclosure, a long, narrow cylinder. A coffin—

She was having the nightmare she'd had at the cabin. Battling the scream that rose in her throat, she tried to convince herself she was dreaming. But it didn't wash. She was fully conscious now, and terror turned her blood to ice.

She knew almost at once where she was. Dawson had put her in the coffin that had been shipped to FAHIL two days ago. She had no idea what he'd done with the bones of the hundred-year-old bride...unless they were still in the coffin, too. Unless Erin was lying beside the skeleton.

Bones can't hurt you. She'd worked with remains for years. Nothing to be afraid of.

What she truly had to fear was the lack of oxygen. Already, she was having a difficult time breathing. The air was heavy and toxic, and every time she drew in a breath, her lungs exploded in pain.

Smoke. She smelled smoke. The coffin wasn't airtight. Somehow it must have been damaged when the bulldozer had dug it up. Now smoke rushed through the tiny holes, and within moments, Erin would not be able to breathe at all.

She beat on the coffin, struggled to push the heavy lid aside, but her strength waned by the second. She couldn't get out. She was trapped. The lab would burn with her inside, and she would never know the identity of Case 00-04.

Would Erin's bones remain unidentified as well? Would anyone even think to look for her inside the coffin, or would they assume the bones that would be turned to ash by the fire were those of the ancient bride?

No, she thought. Nick wouldn't let that happen. He'd search high and low for her. He'd find her no matter what. He'd come looking for her even though she was an O'Roarke, even though they were supposed to be enemies, even though he no longer trusted her.

"Nick!" she tried to call hoarsely. "Help me!"

"Erin? Where are you?"

She thought for a moment the voice was her imagination, but almost at once, the coffin lid was wrenched open and strong arms lifted her out. The lab was full of smoke, too, and Erin coughed and sputtered as her rescuer set her gently on the floor.

"Do you know how to open the emergency exit? That's the quickest way out of here."

She nodded. The air was so thick she could barely see his face, but she realized he wasn't Nick. He sounded like Nick. He reminded her of Nick. But he wasn't Nick.

"Who are you?" she managed to gasp.

"Come on," he said. "We have to get you out of here."

He helped her across the lab to the emergency door, and Erin, holding her shirt to her nose and mouth, punched in the code. The man drew back the door, letting in a blast of fresh air as a frantic voice shouted behind them.

"Erin? Oh, God, are you in here?"

It *was* Nick's voice this time. She tried to call out to him, but her throat and lungs were burning.

"Over here," she called weakly, but she was almost certain he couldn't hear her.

A draft from the open emergency door parted the smoke for a moment, and she saw Nick heading toward her. He scooped her up and carried her outside as the smoke billowed from the open doorway.

He carried her down the alley as sirens screamed

somewhere behind them. "Russell is still in there," she croaked.

Nick laid her down gently. "Are you sure?"

"He was unconscious—"

Before Erin could finish, Nick was up and running back toward the lab. The emergency door was still open, and Erin saw Nick plunge back inside. Her heart pounded in terror. If anything happened to Nick because of her…oh, God…

Within seconds, she saw him dragging Russell Quay outside. The man was still unconscious, and Erin struggled to her feet, staggering toward them.

"He's alive," Nick said. "But we'd better find the paramedics."

"What about your father?" she rasped.

"The remains are destroyed," he said grimly.

"That's not what I mean." Erin grabbed at his arm almost frantically. "He saved me. Your father saved me. He was inside the lab."

"You're in shock," Nick said, wrapping his jacket around her shoulders. "Just sit here with Quay and let me go find the paramedics.

Erin clutched fistfuls of shirt, drawing him to her. "I saw him, Nick. I swear it. Your father is alive."

SHE WAS obviously delusional and in need of medical attention, but she was putting up one hell of a fight. Every time the paramedic tried to put the oxygen mask over her face, she'd shove away his hand. "No! You have to listen to me!"

Finally the paramedic gave up, and joined his partner who was working on Russell. Erin sat up and shrugged out of Nick's jacket. "You have to listen to me, Nick.

I know who killed Ashley. It wasn't Daniel. He was framed.''

"Erin—"

"No!" She grabbed his hand, gripping his fingers so tightly Nick winced.

"I know who the real killer is! He set fire to the lab tonight, and he almost killed me, too. It's Dawson, Nick. Ed Dawson. He told me everything."

Fear tingled through Nick's bloodstream even as he tried to convince himself Erin was still delusional. But her eyes were clear. Her expression almost calm.

"He told me everything, Nick. He killed Ashley with Daniel's knife. That's why Daniel's fingerprints were on the murder weapon. That's why he assigned your father to head the investigation, because he knew the hatred between our two families would make Sean go after Daniel. But then Sean started having doubts about Daniel's guilt. He started to suspect Dawson, and Dawson shot him. *Shot* him, Nick. There was no bullet wound in the remains we recovered. That man wasn't your father. Sean Gallagher is still alive. I saw him—"

Nick grasped Erin's shoulders, gazing down at her almost savagely. "He's not alive. He can't be." Fear flickered in Erin's eyes, and Nick released her at once, cursing himself for frightening her. "I'm sorry."

"No, it's okay," she said softly. "I understand. Maybe it was only a vision I saw. Some kind of hallucination. But I didn't imagine Ed Dawson. He was in the lab, Nick. He tried to kill me."

"My mother has a date with him tonight," Nick said on a wave of his own fear. "He could be with her right now."

SOME MONTHS AGO, Ed Dawson had moved out of the swanky lakeside high-rise he'd shared with his second

wife, Annette, and was now residing in a chic bunga-
low near Lincoln Park. Maggie Gallagher had only
been to his home once before, but she'd memorized the
layout, and now she moved silently and unerringly
through the darkened rooms to the bedroom.

There had to be evidence here. After all these
years—such a long separation—she wouldn't entertain
even the slightest doubt that everything she and Sean
had sacrificed had been in vain.

Dawson had gotten away with murder for eight long
years, but no more, Maggie vowed silently. Somehow,
some way she would find the evidence she needed to
prove that he had not only killed Ashley, but—

A soft tapping at the sliding glass door in the bedroom stilled her heart for a moment until she recognized the shadow outside. She slipped across the room
and slid the door back. The pungent aroma of smoke
drifted in with the tall, broad-shouldered man who embraced her briefly.

"What happened?" Maggie whispered in fear. "I
smell smoke."

"It's okay," Sean Gallagher told her. "He set the
lab on fire, but everyone got out safe."

Maggie's breath quickened. "Erin?"

"She's okay, but she saw him, Maggie. She can put
him away. We don't have to do this. In fact, we need
to get out of here."

He urged her across the room, but before Maggie
could slip into the hallway, a hand locked around her
neck as the overhead light came on.

Sean blinked and reach for his gun, but Dawson said
coolly, "Don't even try it, Sean. Just drop the gun."
When Sean hesitated, his grip tightened around Mag-

gie's throat. Dots swam before her eyes. "Do it!" he all but screamed. "Or I'll kill her right here and now. I swear it."

The gun fell from Sean's hand, and the pressure on Maggie's windpipe lessened. She drew in a series of painful breaths.

"So," Dawson said. "You had your own little agenda, eh, Maggie?"

"You didn't actually think I was in love with you," she gasped.

His arm tightened slightly. "As a matter of fact, I did, but then, I also thought you were a widow." His gaze moved to Sean. "It's an understatement to say that I'm surprised to see you."

Sean gave a short, bitter laugh. "I can imagine. I've waited eight long years to see that look on your face."

"Eight years is a long time to wait just to die again," Dawson said. He leveled his gun at Sean's chest, and Maggie's legs buckled in terror.

NICK PARKED his car a block from Dawson's house and turned to stare at Erin in the darkness. "Are you sure you're okay? I still think I should have taken you to the hospital."

"I'm fine," Erin said. "The important thing now is to find your mother."

Nick nodded. "Okay. Just stay here and lock the doors."

"Shouldn't you call for backup?" Erin hated to think of him walking into Ed Dawson's house alone. Not after coming face-to-face with Dawson herself.

"And tell them what? I suspect the superintendent is a murderer? How many officers do you think would show up to bail me out, Erin?"

She saw his point. "Okay, but be careful." When he started to get out of the car, she caught his arm again. "Nick?"

When he turned, she shrugged lightly.

"Just Nick?" he said with a slight smile.

Her heart turned over at that smile. "I'm sorry I didn't tell you the truth."

"I'm sorry for a lot of things, Erin. But now isn't the time to sort all that out."

"I know."

He reached over and brushed her lips with his. "Lock the doors."

And then he was gone before Erin had time to catch her breath.

LIGHT SPILLED from the sliding glass door at the back of the house, and Nick kept to the shadows as he slipped along the wall. He could hear voices, male and female, and as he peered through the open door, adrenaline—and fear—rushed through his veins.

His mother was inside, locked against Dawson who was armed. Nick's hand tightened around his own weapon. He braced himself but he didn't have a clean shot. He couldn't risk hitting his mother.

"Damn." He willed his mother to move just an inch either way. He tried to reposition himself for the shot, but as he moved to the other side of the door, he realized there was a third person in the room. He froze, his heart thundering, when he heard the man's voice.

"The evidence was just a little too convenient," Sean Gallagher was saying. "Oh, I bought it at first. I was just as eager as anyone to pin the blame on Daniel O'Roarke, but then after a while I got to thinking that maybe there was someone else out there who had a stronger motivation than Daniel. It was nothing concrete, just a gut feeling that I'd arrested the wrong man. I came to you and Liam with my doubts, remember? And after that, I started getting the phone calls. The threats against my boys. Then I got a picture of Fiona, slashed in the same places Ashley had been stabbed.

"I tried to convince myself the O'Roarkes were behind it. That's why I went on that fishing trip alone that weekend, even though you and Liam were supposed to go with me. I needed time to think, figure things out. Only, you didn't want me thinking, did you, Ed? You didn't want me figuring things out."

Dawson gave a little shrug. "I followed you up there. I knew you wouldn't let it go until you had it all worked out. I waited until you came out of the cabin, and then I shot you. It was a clean shot. Caught you right in the chest. You weren't breathing," he said almost in wonder. "You were dead. So I dug a hole and buried you, thinking I'd seen the last of you. Then Roy Glass called and said they'd found some remains near your cabin." He paused, his expression hardening. "So, you dug yourself out of your own grave, Sean. Where've you been all these years? What kind of man lets his family think he's dead for eight long years?"

Nick's heart pounded sickeningly. He felt almost dizzy as he lifted a hand to wipe the sweat from his eyes. His father was alive. All these years...the grief...the loneliness...the rage...

"I was in bad shape for a long time," Sean said. I made it across the border, and a buddy I knew in Canada put me up for a while until I could get myself back together, try to figure things out. By the time I was able to get around, I realized that my instincts had been right. Daniel O'Roarke didn't kill Ashley. The real murderer was still out there, and if he knew I was still alive, he'd come after my family to flush me out. My boys were all on the force by then, and you and I both know how easy it is to kill a cop on the streets. Fiona had already been threatened. All I could do was lay low until I could figure out who the real killer was. I just didn't think it would take eight years to do it.''

''And what about you?'' Dawson's arm tightened around Maggie's throat. His eyes gleamed like cold steel in the bedroom light. ''I take it you weren't as surprised to see him here as I was.''

''I've known for a long time he was alive,'' she said softly.

Nick closed his eyes briefly. His mother had known. All these years, she'd let Nick think his father was dead...she'd let him believe the worst...

He loved his family so much. Everything he did was for us. He always tried to protect us.

And now it was Nick's turn. He shook off the anger and sense of betrayal as he steadied the weapon in his hand.

''I'm sorry, Maggie. Truly sorry I have to do this.'' Dawson's finger tightened on the trigger. Nick lunged forward just as Erin appeared in the doorway behind Dawson. He swung around, firing wildly. Somehow Maggie struggled free, and as she fell to the floor, Nick took Dawson down with one shot.

Chapter Fifteen

Nick glanced around his mother's crowded living room. It had been three days since Ed Dawson's death, and he'd barely had time to catch his breath, let alone stop and sort out his feelings. He'd been interrogated and interviewed almost round the clock for the first twenty-four hours, then the subsequent forty-eight hours had been spent giving endless statements and depositions and avoiding reporters. His face had been plastered all over the news. He hadn't expected to walk away unscathed, but the media onslaught had been almost overwhelming.

But then, it wasn't every day the superintendent of the police department was shot and killed by one of his own men. A detective who claimed the superintendent was a murderer. A cop whose father had miraculously risen from the dead to corroborate the story.

Nick drew a long breath, still not certain he understood everything himself. He wasn't sure he ever would. His father had been alive all these years, and his mother had known for at least the last two years. But she'd never dropped a hint, never given a clue. Nick paused, remembering the night he'd come over to sit on the steps, how certain he'd been then that his father was nearby. Nick had almost caught him slipping out of the house that night.

A hand fell on his shoulder, and Nick turned.

"How's it going?"

It was the first time since the case had broken that Nick and John had been alone. Nick stared at his brother now, a myriad of emotions rising inside him. The resentment, the anger—all of it had been misplaced. All of it had been for nothing. Bitter regret welled inside Nick. "You knew he was alive all along."

John shook his head, his own blue eyes shadowed with emotion. "I didn't know. I was as much in the dark as you were, Nick."

"I've been a real son of a bitch to you at times," Nick said. "I'm sorry."

John's smile was a little sad. "We've all had a hard time. But now's not the time for looking back."

"Maybe not," Nick said. "But eight years is a long time. It's hard to forget all that pain. Hard to get past it, you know?"

John nodded. "Yeah. But would we have done any differently in his place? I don't know. But I do know one thing. He did what he did for us, and he never left us. He's been right here the whole time, watching over us."

"As Fisher," Nick said.

John grinned suddenly. "You've got to give him credit. He was one hell of an informant."

Nick couldn't help grinning, too. "He was always one hell of a cop, too."

"Still is. He brought down Dawson, didn't he? With a little help from you."

"And from Mom."

"And from Erin. Where is she, by the way?"

Nick hadn't seen Erin in three days. Not because he hadn't wanted to, but because she'd been avoiding him. She hadn't returned any of his calls, and when he'd gone by her apartment, she hadn't been home. Nick had no idea where she'd gone off to, but he suspected she was trying to give him time to come to terms with what had happened. He'd thought her brother was a murderer all these years, had been prepared to do everything in his power to send Daniel back to prison. Maybe she just plain didn't want to see a man, a cop, who had been that blind to the truth.

Maybe she'd decided she wanted no part of any of the Gallaghers. After everything that had happened, Nick wasn't sure he could blame her.

"Well," John said, as his grasp tightened on Nick's shoulder. "We've never claimed to be the Waltons, have we?"

TWILIGHT HAD FALLEN, but Erin made no move to leave. She stood staring at the burned-out shell that was once the Forensic Anthropology and Human Identification Lab. Her dream.

It was gone now. Nothing left but a pile of rubble and ashes. And though FAHIL could be rebuilt, case 00-04 might never be solved. It pained Erin to think the man's family might be out there somewhere, wondering what happened to him, still waiting for him to come home.

She turned away at last, and noticed, without surprise, that a car had pulled to the curb behind her, a long, black Mercedes that she recognized at once. The back door opened, and Dylan O'Roarke stepped out.

He strode over to her, taking her hand in his and squeezing it lightly. "How are you doing, Irish?"

She didn't bother to correct him. After all, she'd gotten to know Dylan and her father both a little better during the last three days. She was willing to accept that a part of her was and always would be Irish O'Roarke if they were willing to accept that her one and true identity was Erin Casey.

"Have you seen Nick?" he asked her.

Erin shrugged. "No."

"Don't let this thing drag on, Erin. You two need to talk, sort things out."

Erin wasn't sure they could sort things out. Even though Daniel had been cleared, she was still an O'Roarke. A lot of bitterness still simmered between their two families. Loyalties would always be divided.

"Talk to him," Dylan urged.

"I will."

He nodded. "In the meantime, there's someone who wants to see you."

Erin cast a glance toward the car. "My father—"

But the tall man who climbed from the back of the car wasn't Richard O'Roarke. He was younger, thin to the point of gauntness. His dark-blond hair was a bit too long and much too shaggy, but the moment he lifted his gaze to Erin, everything inside her stilled.

"Daniel?"

He came slowly toward her. "It's been a long time," he said in a deep, liquid voice. A beautiful voice that seemed almost incongruent with his shabby appearance.

"It's been forever," Erin said, and walked quite naturally into her brother's arms.

NICK WAS WAITING for her on the steps outside her apartment. He rose when she came around the corner, and Erin felt at once awkward and unsure of herself. So much had happened in the past few days. So many things lay unsettled between them.

He looked as uncertain as she felt, which gave Erin a measure of strength. He shoved his hands in his pockets, gazing down at her.

"I just saw my brother," Erin said. "Dylan told me that you and your father helped cut through the red tape to get him released."

Nick shrugged. "It was the least we could do. Believe it or not, I'm glad he's free, Erin. All I ever wanted was justice."

"I know that."

"Do you?" He gazed at her intently. "I'm sorry I ever doubted you. You didn't deserve that. You're one of the most honorable people I've ever known."

Her heart quickened at his tone, at his words. "I can understand why you had doubts." The wind off the lake was getting sharp, and Erin wrapped her arms around her middle. "So many things were put into motion before you and I were ever born. This thing between our families—it's a lot to get past, Nick."

He lifted a hand to touch her hair. "I used to think it was impossible. There was a time when an O'Roarke would have been the last person I'd want to be involved with."

"And now?"

"I can't imagine wanting anyone else." He caught her face in both his hands. "I'm in love with you, Erin."

Tears sprang to her eyes. "Are you sure? My name

is Casey now, but that doesn't change the fact that I was born with the name O'Roarke.''

He smiled at her tenderly. ''Yeah, but I'm kind of hoping that someday soon you might consider changing it to Gallagher.''

Silhouette Stars

Born this Month

Don McLean, Buster Keaton, Clive James, Paul Hogan, Sean Lennon, Cliff Richard, Margaret Thatcher, Max Bygraves, Bill Gates, Bob Hoskins

Star of the Month

Libra

The next few months should prove challenging, you will need your wits about you and the support of those close to you. However, you will begin to feel that real progress is possible in your life and long held dreams can become reality. Finance looks good and there may be a chance for long distance travel later in the year.

SILH/HR/0010a

 **Scorpio**

A great month for relationships, you will feel stronger and more committed, by being honest with your partner you will achieve new heights.

Sagittarius

Life remains complicated and you need to sort out your priorities. Loved ones will be able to support you but only if you show real appreciation.

 **Capricorn**

You're in demand both socially and at work, you may find you need to simplify your life in order to keep everybody happy and you sane!

Aquarius

Time to sort out your priorities, by trying to please everyone you are not really achieving much. Travel plans may have to be changed at the last minute.

 Pisces

You should be feeling optimistic about the way your life is going, especially in relationships where you realise just how much you mean to that special person.

Aries

Your natural charm enables you to win over friends and colleagues to your way of thinking making this month one of progress in many areas of your life. A shopping trip could find you bargain hunting with style.

Taurus

You may feel unmotivated and not so sure where your life is heading; don't despair, changes are just around the corner. Financial matters improve and you may receive something material from an unusual source.

Gemini

There are many positive aspects around you and by being confident you can succeed in all you desire, making this an excellent month. A friend has news that sets you thinking about how loyal someone close is.

 Cancer

You could be fighting to find some personal space as the demands from work and socially get too much. Sift out the important and allow the rest to drop away, leaving you time to refresh.

Leo

You should be revelling in the attention you are receiving as a result of recent achievements but deep down you feel that someone close is not being as supportive as you would like. Whatever their motives, now could be truthtime.

Virgo

Romance is highlighted and you will feel pleased with the way a special relationship is going. Finances are looking good and you may splash out later in the month.

© Harlequin Mills & Boon Ltd 2000

Look out for more
Silhouette Stars next month

SILHOUETTE
INTRIGUE™

AVAILABLE FROM 20TH OCTOBER 2000

WANTED: COWBOY Kelsey Roberts

Shadows & Spice!

As the only witness to a murder, Barbara Prather had an assassin on her trail. Her protector, Cade Landry, had kidnapped her to save her life, but was his interest professional...or personal?

UNDER THE MIDNIGHT SUN
Marilyn Cunningham

Malinche Adams came to Brian Kennedy and asked for his help finding her brother's killer. She burrowed into his solitary life with ease—and into his bed with passionate fervour. But there was danger dogging their every step...

LOVE AT FIRST SIGHT BJ Daniels

Lawman Lover

Karen Sutton was convinced she could catch a criminal on her own, but when an accident erased her memory, suddenly her life was in Detective Jack Adams's hands. And Jack would do *anything* to save Karen from danger—even marry her!

SAME PLACE, SAME TIME CJ Carmichael

Detective Morgan Forrester and Trista Emerson had to work together. Once husband and wife, could the hunt for a ruthless killer bring them together again? Sexy Morgan was convinced that Trista might be the next victim...

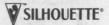

THE MACGREGORS

4 BOOKS ON THIS WELL-LOVED FAMILY

BY

NORA ROBERTS

Book 1 - Serena and Caine - September 2000

Book 2 - Alan and Grant - December 2000

Book 3 - Daniel and Ian - May 2001

Book 4 - Rebellion - August 2001

Don't miss these four fantastic books by Silhouette's top author

2 FREE
books and a surprise gift!

We would like to take this opportunity to thank you for reading this Silhouette® book by offering you the chance to take TWO more specially selected titles from the Desire™ series absolutely FREE! We're also making this offer to introduce you to the benefits of the Reader Service™—

- ★ FREE home delivery
- ★ FREE gifts and competitions
- ★ FREE monthly Newsletter
- ★ Exclusive Reader Service discounts
- ★ Books available before they're in the shops

Accepting these FREE books and gift places you under no obligation to buy, you may cancel at any time, even after receiving your free shipment. Simply complete your details below and return the entire page to the address below. *You don't even need a stamp!*

YES! Please send me 2 free Desire books and a surprise gift. I understand that unless you hear from me, I will receive 4 superb new titles every month for just £2.70 each, postage and packing free. I am under no obligation to purchase any books and may cancel my subscription at any time. The free books and gift will be mine to keep in any case.

D0ZEA

Ms/Mrs/Miss/Mr ....Initials.....................................
BLOCK CAPITALS PLEASE

Surname ....

Address ....

....

....Postcode.................................

Send this whole page to:
UK: FREEPOST CN81, Croydon, CR9 3WZ
EIRE: PO Box 4546, Kilcock, County Kildare (stamp required)